Captured

Nicole Targaryen

ISBN:
ISBN:

Front cover image by Nicole Targaryen
Book design by Nicole Targaryen

www.officialnicoletargaryen.wordpress.com

Acknowledgements

I would like to thank God for all that He has done for me. Though I was upset about it at the time, I am grateful that God put me in situations that motivated me to finish this book. I am even thankful that God made me ill every time I tried to work on a book other than this one. If not for His divine intervention, I may not have ever finished this book.

I would also like to thank my family, who supported and encouraged me no matter what. I am grateful to have such great family members who allowed me to do what I loved, even if it did not seem like the most profitable option.

Finally, I would like to thank the individuals who inspired the scenes and characters in this story. I am grateful to the individuals who created stories and characters which in turn inspired my stories and characters. I would also like to thank my muse.

Table of Contents

Chapter One: From Ai'Windel

This wasn't supposed to be happening, not to us. Our planet was resistant to the Intergalactic Endeavour, but we weren't loud about it like some of the others. Still, we had all been dragged from our homes and forced to kneel in front of a line of soldiers now, despite the lines of fighting protestors. We would be executed any minute now, and my story would end before it had even really begun.

My family and I had already said our goodbyes and final words to each other. We were hopeful when they had first touched down on our planet, but we knew what would happen when we heard the screaming. We had spent what we supposed would be our final moments expressing our love to each other. It did not feel real to me, though, until we were ripped out of our home by the soldiers and forced onto our knees.

"Wait," a soldier held up his arm, "scan this woman."

He pointed to me, and I could see my family looking at me in my peripheral vision. Before I could say anything, I was grabbed and forced to my feet by two other soldiers. Once I was standing, another soldier scanned me from head to toe. They kept me standing for a while, shifting their weight from leg to leg as they stood.

"Affirmative." The soldier holding the scanner nodded.

"You have been chosen to serve the organization." The first soldier, who seemed to be high-ranking, told me.

"And what of my family?" I asked.

"The Intergalactic Endeavour will give your home planet and family whatever you wish to give them." he said.

"Astraella, don't," my mother said, "you don't want to do this."

I was slightly offended by her doubt, but I understood her concern. I had been sheltered and spoiled by my parents for my entire life and even I doubted I could make it in such an extreme work environment. Everything and everyone on Ai'Windel were peaceful and slow; nothing like the Intergalactic Endeavour.

"It's fine, just refuse." My father added.

"I want Ai'Windel to be left in complete peace... no more killings or torturing of any kind," I said, "my family will be left in peace and given enough money to sustain their lifestyles forever."

The soldier with the scanner shrugged and nodded.

"And... I want the Intergalactic Endeavour to donate money to my planet," I added, "to help them rebuild after your attack on them."

The first soldier looked at the soldier with the scanner. He shrugged and nodded once more.

"You two, escort her to the ship," he said, "move out."

He motioned for the rest of the soldiers to follow him. To my surprise, they did exactly as they were commanded. I hadn't expected them to really grant my wishes, but I figured I had to at least try. However, all the soldiers left the people alone and got back onto the ship. The only casualty seemed to be my freedom.

I was escorted without force to the large spaceship in front of us. I glanced back at my family just before I boarded and waved, smiling as brightly as I could manage. The soldiers escorting me allowed me to stay there and wave goodbye to them until the door closed on us.

"We'll take you to your owner's room now." One of the soldiers said.

The thought of having someone own me was enough to make me sick. I had been treated as a princess my entire life and now I would be treated like a slave. I wondered if I would regret my decision once I experienced what those less fortunate than me experienced every day of their lives. But, if they could survive it, why not me?

'At least I will gain a new perspective.' I thought, trying to cheer myself up.

I walked with the two soldiers, one in front of me and one behind me, down the long halls. Soldiers were rushing about around us, either removing or putting on combat gear. They chatted casually with each other and paid me little mind as I made my way through the halls. We stopped outside a shiny grey door, which one of my escorts opened.

"You will stay here until he returns." One of the soldiers informed me.

I entered the room and watched as they closed the doors, locking me in. I had no idea when the man who apparently owned the quarters would be back, so I decided I would at least look around. I did not know if this place would be my new home, but if it was to be, then I wanted to be familiar with it.

I wondered as I explored what my responsibilities would be in this place. There was an office with a conference table and two desks, a kitchen, a bathroom, a rather large closet filled with very few clothes, a bedroom, and a living area with a large couch, a holoprojection machine, and two chairs in the room. Everything was grey and white, and extremely organized. The space was large, which meant that there were probably a hundred tasks that I would have to perform.

I sat on one of the under-stuffed chairs in the living area and tried to guess what my job would be. The place was pristine, so I would probably not be cleaning it. The owner of the space seemed to be single, so I would likely not be babysitting or attending to a wife. Perhaps I would be a chef or a personal assistant for the man. After all, what else would there be for me to do?

I racked my brain for evidence which would point to my position in the organization. I had been scanned from head to toe, meaning that my health and appearance was important. In what field would both my appearance and health be so incredibly important?

I could feel my eyes widen and the blood drain from my face as the most probable explanation popped into my brain. I sunk to the ground, hyperventilating as visions of my future ran through my mind. I pulled my knees to my chest, wrapping my arms around myself. Tears were streaming from my eyes as I rocked back and forth, not even trying to calm myself down.

As I began to feel overwhelmingly anxious, I stood and began to pace around the space. My body shook as I walked through the area, trying to think of a way out of this. I had willingly walked into a situation which very well might traumatize me for the rest of my life and now I had no way out, at least not one in sight.

Heavy footsteps sounded closely to the room's entrance and I froze. I leapt into the small closet in the hallway as I heard the doors opening. As the footsteps sounded closer and closer to me, I tried to slow and quiet my breathing. I held my breath when I heard him enter the room and squeezed my eyes shut. I knew closing my eyes wouldn't help, but it made me feel better.

It took him approximately a minute to find me, which I only knew because I had been counting the seconds in my anxiousness. My eyes widened as I heard him open the door, allowing me to examine him. He was tall, muscular, with dark hair and dark eyes. I was too terrified of what I suspected was to come to decide if he was handsome or not.

"What are you doing here?" He asked, grabbing my arm and yanking me out.

"I was scared." I squeaked.

I immediately felt stupid for having said what I had said. He just frowned down at me, not saying anything or making any sounds to acknowledge my response.

"What do you want me here for?" I inquired quietly after a long, awkward pause.

"Me." He answered, grabbing my wrist.

Had I not been scared; I would have rolled my eyes at his painfully obvious answer. He dragged me to his bedroom, and I felt my body begin to shake once more. Once we were securely inside, he shut the door behind us and let go of my wrist. I watched as he removed his shirt and balled it up in his hand.

"Here," he threw it to me, "I'm going to change... in the closet."

I knew very little about these kinds of things, but I was pretty sure this was not normal for this situation, whether it was forced or consensual. Regardless, I decided that I would remove my clothing and put his shirt on, for fear of the alternative. The shirt fit as a small dress would and was just as comfortable as one might expect a man's t-shirt to be.

He returned not long after I had finished changing and climbed under the covers. I stood on the other side of the bed, too afraid to move. Once he was settled, he turned to look at me, confusion in his eyes.

"Are you going to lay down or...?" He trailed off.

I merely nodded and climbed into bed next to him, too afraid of the consequences if I refused. He turned the lights off and then laid down. I followed suit, staring up at the ceiling and waiting for what I dreaded more than anything. I felt his arm fall across my waist and tensed instinctively.

He pulled me closer to him and wrapped his arm all the way around my waist. It took me a full minute to realize that what I thought was going to occur was not going to. I tried to relax, but still felt uncomfortable sleeping next to the unfamiliar man. Was this truly all that would occur or was this some kind of weird test? Either way, I was incredibly vexed by the situation.

I must have fallen asleep eventually because when I opened my eyes, it had been 5 hours since I had last looked at the clock. My stomach felt odd, as if it were full of water and the water was turning constantly. My throat was tight, and I felt as though if I dared open my mouth, I would expel everything I had eaten that day. These feelings were all too familiar to me.

The strange man's arm was still wrapped tightly around me, making me feel even more nauseous. I attempted to push him off, but he only pulled me closer. I wiggled a bit in order to force him to loosen his grip, then pushed his arm off of me and made a beeline for the bathroom I had explored earlier.

It took me a few seconds to find the light switches and the other amenities in the dark, but as soon as I did, I fell to the floor. I had only enough time to lift the toilet seat and pull my hair back before I vomited. I tried to be quiet so I wouldn't wake and thus upset my companion, or captor, or whatever he was to me, but my efforts proved to be in vain as he soon appeared by my side.

"Are you okay?" He asked as I took a pause.

I fLushed the toilet and wiped my face before answering. Had I not been terrified *and* ill, I would have been embarrassed that he was seeing me like this.

"Not really," I chuckled weakly, "but this happens a lot, so I'm used to it."

"It happens a lot?" He frowned.

"I get stressed really easily," I told him, "So much so that I make myself ill."

"Why were you stressed?" He inquired.

"I was captured by an organization which my family is... not necessarily supportive of," I explained, "and I didn't know what was going to happen to me. Then I was put in this room, and I figured out...well, I thought you were going to rape me."

He furrowed his brows as he looked down at me. I felt like a little child sitting there crumpled up on the floor.

"I'm not going to rape you." He said.

“I know that now,” I responded weakly, trying to force a chuckle, “but I didn’t know that at first, so I was really nervous and stressed and anxious and... all those words.”

We remained in silence for a few moments. I wondered if I should say something, but I couldn’t think of anything else to say.

“Do you want me to help you up?” He asked, “I can get washcloths for you to clean up wit,h or you can take a shower if you want.”
“Just give me a minute to rest, please.” I said.

He nodded and I leaned my head back against the wall. I appreciated his offer, but I just couldn’t get up right now. I closed my eyes for a few moments, trying to assess how I was feeling moment by moment. I eventually figured out that my stomach had expelled all that it needed to, and I opened my eyes again.

“So, why do you want me?” I asked, “just to have someone to sleep next to at night?”

"We work long, hard hours to accomplish our goal," he answered, "we have little time to find romantic partners. I asked the soldiers to keep a lookout for a woman meeting my standards."

"And I did?" I inquired, feeling stupid once I had.

"They scanned you and sent it to me," he continued, "you were perfect for the purpose."

"So, what is my role, then, exactly?" I stammered.

"Keep me company." He shrugged.

"And in return you offer protection for my home planet and family?" I asked.

"Unless they directly attack us." He returned.

"Fair enough." I smiled.

"You seemed rather close with your family, the soldiers said," he stated, "are you still living with them?"

"Yes, I just turned 24," I nodded, "I know it's a bit taboo for people to live with their families after adult age, but I love my family, and I wanted to stay with them."

"What have you been doing in those three years since you became an adult?" He queried, "did you have a lover back home?"

"I didn't," I replied, "people seem... seemed put off by me, I guess. I'm a bit odd, I suppose, and I make them uncomfortable."

"I don't think you're odd." He said.

"Well, then maybe that means you are odd too." I laughed.

He looked a bit hurt, so I placed my hand on his apologetically.

"But...maybe we're the same kind of odd." I added with a reassuring smile.

He smiled, only slightly, but enough to raise my spirits. In the short time I had been here, he had not smiled once, and it frightened me. Now, I felt just slightly more comfortable with him.

"Will you help me up now, slowly?" I asked.

He nodded and offered me his hands. I took them and allowed him to pull me up, even slower than I had actually needed. It was rare that someone knew what I needed after such a sickness; even my family members had needed to learn exactly what to do.

"Are you okay?" He inquired, studying my face diligently.

"I think so," I answered, "can I have that washcloth now? And maybe some mouthwash?"

He turned and retrieved both items for me, his eyes barely leaving me. I timidly rinsed my mouth with the mouthwash before washing my face off with the washcloth.

"Is there anything else you need?" He asked, "tea? Honey for your throat? A bath? Some blankets?"

"Um, do you have a really fluffy blanket?" I inquired shyly, "I really like to wrap up in a fluffy blanket after I get sick. It calms me down."

"I can go find one," he said, "it might take me longer since there's fewer soldiers on duty right now."

"Oh, it's okay, don't worry about it." I replied.

"I don't mind, I want you to feel comfortable," he said, "let me help you back to bed and I'll go find one."

He escorted me back to the bed, making sure to go slowly. Once I was safely back in bed, I watched him leave the bedroom. I heard the front doors open and curled up into a ball while I waited for him to return.

I had always thought that I would be resistant to the infamous Stockholm Syndrome if I were ever imprisoned, but now I was not so sure. Of course, I had no romantic feelings for the man, but my feelings toward him were more friendly than hateful. He seemed kind, and thus far he had not prevented me from doing anything I wanted or forced me to do anything. He was kind and considerate, and he seemed like he genuinely cared about me.

The front doors opened once more, alerting me that the man was back. He stumbled into the bedroom carrying a huge, white, faux fur blanket. He dropped it onto the bed and looked down at me.

"Does this work?" He asked, "it was the closest thing I could find to a 'fluffy blanket.'"

"It's perfect," I grinned, "thank you."

I pulled the blanket around my shoulders and pulled my knees to my chest. As the man rejoined me in bed, I leaned my head up against the headboard. I felt much calmer and safer now.

"Is it alright if I put my arm around you?" He inquired.

"You practically pinned me to you all night and now you ask for permission?" I laughed.

"You're sick now." He shrugged.

"You can if you want." I replied.

He scooted next to me and put his arm around my shoulders. I felt warm and safe, despite having been captured by him less than half a day ago. The blanket was soft, and his arms provided a comforting weight which soon Lulled me into a deep sleep.

When I woke up, I was laying horizontally across the bed, and I was alone. I could hear noises from the bathroom and stretched out on the bed, assuming my captor was preparing to leave for the day. After a few minutes, the door opened, and I turned my head towards the sound.

"How are you feeling?" he asked.

"Fine, I guess." I replied, stretching my arms above my head.

"You will stay here until I return," he told me, "You can order food on the tablet in the kitchen and it will be brought to you. I'm having clothes made for you, but until then you can borrow mine."

"Why can't I leave?" I questioned.

"I don't want you causing chaos," he replied, "I don't trust you yet."

I raised my eyebrows at him and sat up to face him.

"You don't trust *me*?" I scoffed, "last time I checked, I was the prisoner here."

"You came aboard willingly, did you not?" he questioned.

"Well, yes, but..." I began.

"And have you been denied anything necessary to your survival?" he interrogated, "have you been caged or treated as a prisoner?"

"You won't let me leave." I pouted, crossing my arms over my chest.

"Without me." He countered, leaning forward.

I wrinkled my nose at him and collapsed back onto the bed. I wasn't really as peeved as I pretended to be, I just enjoyed messing with him, mostly because I liked the way his eyebrows knitted together.

"Is there anything else you need or would like?" he asked,

"Workout equipment?" I answered.

"I'll take you to the ship's gym after dinner tonight." He said.

"Do you have anything for me to do?" I queried, "like cleaning equipment so I can clean up or something?"

"They'll clean up while we're at the gym," he said, "there's books and tablets and a holoprojection machine."

He was certainly meeting all of my needs, but it didn't fix the problem I was thinking of.

"Are you going to be back soon?" I grumbled, "I'm going to be bored out of my mind."

"Well, what do you usually do at home?" he asked.

"Workout." I replied.

"And?" he pressed.

"And sit on my holocomputer." I mumbled.

"I'll have a new holocomputer delivered for you." He chuckled.

"Am I getting paid for any of this?" I asked, rolling over on my stomach.

"You and your family will be given everything you need for your lifetimes," he said, "I think that is sufficient payment, don't you?"

"Do I even get to go home and see my family?" I questioned.

"Later, if I feel I can trust you," he answered, "I'll be back around 1800 or so."

He smiled only slightly before turning on his heel and leaving me alone. I groaned and faceplanted into the soft sheets.

Chapter Two: A New Home

Despite my firm belief that nothing my so-called owner had in his closet would fit me, I decided to explore his closet once more. After a few minutes of searching and trying on his clothes, I decided on forcing one of his long-sleeved to serve as another very short dress. The shortness of it would have annoyed me in any other situation, but I was unbothered since I was locked in a room all by myself with no one to look at me.

As soon as I felt that I was somewhat clean and presentable, I ordered breakfast on the tablet in the kitchen. While I waited for it to be delivered, I explored my new home for the second time in the 24 hours I had been here. This time, I was looking less at the space and more for something to do while my captor was out.

I tapped on a few of the tablets in the office, trying to find one which had not been matched to another person. Once I found one, I matched it to myself and went to the notepad app. Bored now that my task had been completed, I used the tablet's pen to write out a list of things that I could possibly do while I was locked up all day.

"Astraella's List of Things To Do," I read aloud as I typed, "One – play on tablet, two – read, three – use holocomputers in office (maybe), four – watch stuff on the holoprojection machine (maybe), five – sleep, six – eat, seven – try to work out (without equipment?), and number eight – scream."

After finishing a list that was as short as my so-called dress, I decided to go back to the kitchen to check on the status of my breakfast. Instead of a status update, though, I was greeted with a plate of food on the table in the dining room. I frowned and looked around, wondering who had delivered it and when. No one was in sight, so I sat down and ate in peace, worrying only that someone had heard me talking to myself.

I propped the tablet up on the table, chose a show, and began watching it as I ate my breakfast. I certainly felt lonely as I ate, but I was also grateful for the time alone. I knew very little about the man with whom I was now living, and I felt more comfortable with him not watching my every move.

Once I had finished my breakfast, I dumped the dishes into the dish return for sanitation. I checked the time, only to be disappointed. It was only 07:30, meaning that I still had several hours to occupy myself. Feeling rather tired, I decided to complete the fifth item on my list.

I woke up only 3 hours later, feeling slightly more well-rested but still just as bored. I played on the tablet for a while, then got out of bed and went to the office I had explored earlier. There were two holocomputers, and four laptops in the room, all of which I attempted to use and all of which informed me that I could not use them without an Intergalactic Endeavour Pass. Of course, in such an important organization there would be tight security on all the devices.

I sighed and crossed over to the bench at the other end of the room. The office was set up for both individual work and conferences, making me wonder if others would be coming in and out of these quarters. I also wondered *who* exactly my new owner or companion or whatever was. He had not told me anything about him, not even his rank or his name. I resolved to ask him as soon as he returned, unless I figured it out earlier.

In the meantime, I decided to figure out the holoprojection machine before ordering Lunch. The holoprojection machine was slightly more expensive and nicer than the one I had at home, but it was still easy to figure out. I plopped back on the couch and flipped through the shows, picking one I had never seen before.

After a few episodes, I decided to order Lunch. I went straight back to the couch after ordering, too hooked on the new show to leave for long. The door opened and I turned to see an officer carrying in a tray with my Lunch on it. He simply placed it on the table in the dining room and left the quarters without even acknowledging me.

I chuckled at my quick heartbeat, amused by how anxious I was. As the beating of my heart slowed, I paused the show and crossed to the table. I ate slowly as hundreds of thoughts rushed through my mind, temporarily distracting me from my utter boredom. Unfortunately for me, the kitchen's tablet was right above the dish return, tempting me to order some snacks for my next binge session on the couch. I eventually gave into the temptation and made a quick run to the bathroom.

The food was already waiting for me on the table when I returned from the bathroom. I cheerfully grabbed my snacks and headed back over to the couch for the next few episodes of my new show. I already felt at home here, cuddled up on the comfy couch surrounded by snacks. The only things that were missing were my family and my holocomputer.

"Have you been there all day?" a man's voice sounded, startling me.

I turned quickly to see my companion strolling into the living room. It was both surprising and unsurprising to me that I did not yet recognize his voice.

"Back already?" I chuckled.

"I've been gone 12 hours." He frowned.

I frowned back at him and checked the time on my tablet.

"It's 1800?" I exclaimed.

"Have you had dinner yet?" he asked.

"Nope." I answered, hopping up from the couch.

"Here." He placed a plate on the table.

I sat down opposite him at the kitchen table and began eating with him. He stood once I was done eating and removed our plates from the table.

"Go find something in my closet you can work out in." he commanded.

I retreated to the living room to clean up my things first, a small act of either defiance or procrastination; I wasn't sure which. As soon as I was done, I retreated to the closet to attempt to find workout-worthy clothes. There wasn't much for me to wear, but I was able to find a pair of shorts with a drawstring and a t-shirt. I tightened the shorts as far as they would go and draped the shirt over the rest of my body. The man chuckled when he saw me emerge from the closet.

"Are you ready to go?" he asked, looking me up and down.

"I suppose," I sighed, "I hope you've ordered me workout clothes."

"Workout clothes, pajamas, lounging clothes," he listed, "evening wear, casual wear, you name it."

"Thorough.... that's unusual for a man." I teased.

"Is it?" he returned, "shall we go? We've only got about 3 hours until sundown."

"Yeah." I nodded.

I followed him out of the room and down a small, closed-in hallway. It was crowded with soldiers, hurrying past us. We walked into a larger hallway, which was covered on either side with windows. I gazed in amazement out of them, at the vastness and beauty of space. I hadn't traveled in space before, only around my own planet.

"It's beautiful." I noted.

"Isn't it?" he returned.

He turned down another hallway and into a door on the right. I followed after him and saw before us an empty gym.

"It's awfully quiet, isn't it?" I chuckled.

"I've reserved it until sundown," he replied, "I wanted it later, but the soldiers start training then."

"They let you reserve it?" I asked, "I'm impressed."

"I *am* in command of the entire organization," he shrugged, "so I should be able to reserve the ship's gym once in a while...at least that's my belief."

My eyes widened in surprise as I realized what he meant. If he truly meant that he was in command of the entire organization and wasn't just messing with me, then he was the highest-ranking member in the Intergalactic Endeavour: the Supreme Commander. If he was Supreme Commander, and I was his companion, I was, theoretically, by association, in control of the entire galaxy.

"Are you going to...just sit there?" he asked, "or are you going to work out?"

"Oh right, sorry," I said, "I got distracted."

I hopped onto an exercise simulation board and chose my program. I tried my best to focus on the workouts the simulation board was putting me through, but I couldn't stop myself from looking over at him. I grunted in frustration, wishing in vain that I could focus on my own workout instead of him.

Despite my distraction, I was given a fairly good score on my workout, just like usual. I grabbed a cooling towel from the rack and walked over to my companion, who had finished a few minutes before me. He looked over me with an amused expression and I suddenly felt extremely self-conscious.

"Are you ready to go?" he asked.

"Yeah." I nodded

"Did you have a good workout?" he asked as we walked down the eerily empty halls.

"I guess," I shrugged, "did you?"

"Yep." He replied, an amused smile on his lips.

"What?" I frowned.

He shook his head and chuckled as he stepped into his, or rather *our,* quarters.

"Seriously, what?" I asked as the door closed behind me.

"You didn't seem too focused on your workout." He smirked.

"Oh?" I replied.

"Were you copying mine?" he asked, "or were you just watching me?"

My eyes widened and my cheeks heated, revealing my embarrassment to him. I frowned as soon as I realized my face was betraying me.

"Well, how would you know I was looking at you unless you were looking at me?" I retorted.

"You're a young woman from an enemy planet on *my* spaceship," he said, "of course I was watching you."

I rolled my eyes at him.

"Did you like what you saw?" he teased.

"I just want to know who you are." I huffed.

"Supreme Commander Matticas Damiran." He answered.

"So, you are him." I breathed.

"Him?" he asked.

"You're the Supreme Commander." I said.

"I am." He replied.

"Holy crap," I squeaked, collapsing on the couch, "I'm with the freaking Supreme Commander of the Intergalactic Endeavour."

"Well...did you think a normal officer would have such nice rooms?" he asked.

"I... I don't know!" I exclaimed, "I've never been on a spaceship before."

"You...you've never been in space?" he asked, his brows furrowed.

"No... I've only ever been on Ai'Windel." I responded sheepishly.

"Hmm," he said, "I guess we'll have to travel sometime then."

"You'd take me traveling? Around the galaxy?" I asked.

He nodded in response, and I felt my heart beat faster.

"I thought I was just an employee," I said, "just some...employee who kept you company at night."

"You're my companion, officially," he replied, "and just because you're technically working doesn't mean that I don't want to treat you well."

"What I'm hearing is that you're going to treat me as your girlfriend." I smiled.

"Companion." He corrected.

"Officially," I shrugged, "but...this seems more like I'm your girlfriend."

"You're not my girlfriend." He retorted.

My stomach dropped in disappointment, but I didn't want to reveal my emotions once more, so I simply shrugged and headed off towards the bathroom. I showered and changed into another one of Commander Damiran's shirts, already starting to get annoyed by my lack of clothing options. He followed suit as I jumped back onto the large, comfortable bed. I snuggled into the blanket that he had retrieved for me the night before and waited for him to return from his shower.

I did not wait long for him to return to the bedroom. I stared at him expectantly as he milled about the room, folding clothing and putting various items in their proper places. He seemed to ignore my gaze as he did so; either that or he truly did not notice my eyes on him.

"Is something wrong?" he asked after a few moments.

"What am I to call you?" I returned, "Supreme Commander? Commander Damiran? Commander Matticas?"

"My family and friends called me Matt." He answered.

"And?" I pressed.

"And you may call me Matt," he said, "in informal situations."

I sighed contentedly and leaned back in the bed.

"Oh, I wish my family could see this," I said, "me, in the Supreme Commander of the Intergalactic Endeavour's bed, calling him Matt."

He cocked an eyebrow at me, and I suddenly realized how awkward my sentence had sounded. I cleared my throat as I searched for something less awkward to say.

"I feel like a princess." I giggled.

"Technically speaking, you'd be closer to a queen or empress," he said, "and I thought you said you were a *prisoner.*"

"And you said I wasn't." I retorted.

He frowned at me, then shook his head.

"You're crazy, is what you are." He joked.

I only chuckled in response. His tablet beeped and he picked it up, breaking our conversation. He tapped for a few moments, read over something, then put it back down.

"Your clothes will be delivered tomorrow morning." He told me.

"And what about the holocomputer I was promised?" I asked.

"Same thing...tomorrow morning." He replied.

"I thought you said it would be here today." I said.

"They didn't have one ready for you." He shrugged.

"Will you get me anything I want?" I inquired cheerfully, "since you're the Supreme Commander and all?"

I propped myself up on my elbow and raised an eyebrow at him, trying to look sultry and confident. I only hoped that my words had sounded playful and not needy and spoiled.

"I told you I would," he responded, "and aren't you... or weren't you against the Intergalactic Endeavour?"

"I don't really know," I shrugged, "but I'm having fun with this situation."

"I'm disappointed." He said.

"What do you mean?" I frowned.

"You're more like other people than I thought you might be," he replied, "I thought from your planet's characteristics and yours, you wouldn't be."

"How so? And what's wrong with that, anyway?" I asked.

"As soon as someone is high-ranking or rich, you're all impressed."

He said.

I folded my arms over my chest and furrowed my brows at him.

"I was impressed by you before," I argued, "I just like that your position can offer me...certain benefits."

He hummed in acknowledgement and slipped into the bed next to me. I realized that I had revealed too much to him, and quickly tried to move on.

"So?" I pressed.

"So, what?" he asked.

"You're not disappointed anymore?" I inquired.

"Come closer to me." He commanded before turning out the lights.

I obeyed his command and felt his arm wrap around my waist. I knew that I had won him over, at least for now.

“Can you get me a crown?” I giggled.

“Go to sleep.” He grumbled.

I giggled again but acquiesced to his wishes. Ideas flooded my dreams during the night, filling me with adrenaline. When I was awoken the next morning by voices in the living room, I felt more energized than I had felt in a long time.

“Yes, I’ve got it from here, thank you.” Matt’s voice sounded from the living room.

I heard the main door slide shut and then Matt’s footsteps coming closer to me. I hurriedly sat up in the bed, throwing the blanket off my bare legs. He finally entered the room and looked up at me with less interest than I had hoped.

“Sorry, I was trying not to wake you.” He said nonchalantly.

“That’s alright,” I replied, smiling mischievously, “what were you doing?”

He gave me an odd look and I suddenly felt very self-conscious. Perhaps 8 in the morning was not the best time to work my charm on him.

"Your stuff has been delivered," he told me, "I'm going to grab my stuff and head out to work."

"Are you sure you don't want to stay here with me?" I asked, crawling towards him.

I had never tried to seduce a man into doing my bidding, but my dreams had filled me with the confidence to try. His expression, however, was slowly draining my confidence. The only thing that urged me to keep going was the way that he gulped as he looked down at me.

"I need to go to work." He said, turning and leaving abruptly.

I chuckled to myself before getting up to get ready for the day. After breakfast, I took it upon myself to sort through the things that Matt had gotten me. The wardrobe he had ordered was immense, much too much for me to try on in a single day. Instead of trying to do so, I put on a lounging outfit and set up my new holocomputer.

Since I knew that Matt would probably take me to the gym to work out once again, I focused only on having fun and eating as much as I wanted to. The food that the Intergalactic Endeavour served was much better than the food on Ai'Windel, most likely because they had more resources than we had.

Matt stormed into his quarters at the end of the day, startling me out of my holoprogram-induced trance. I watched from the couch as he looked around the room, as if he was searching for something. When his eyes finally met mine, he stomped towards me and sat down on the couch beside me.

"You okay?" I asked.

"No, Astraella, I'm not," he sighed, "I've had an awful day."

This was the first time I had heard him say my name. To be honest, I hadn't been completely sure that he had known my name until now.

"Tell me about it." I said, scooting closer to him.

Matt exhaled and slid down so that his head was in my lap. He started talking about his workday, most of which I didn't understand. I simply made comments as needed and mindlessly ran my fingers through his dark hair. His hair was distractingly soft, unharmed by harsh suns or weather.

"I mean, maybe it's because everyone was so mean to me in school." He sighed, finishing his rant.
"Wait, what?" I frowned.

Everything else he had said had been rather uninteresting, but this particular sentence piqued my interest. Matt sat up abruptly, as if he was trying to protect the vulnerability I had just latched onto.

"I just think that maybe the reason I'm so concerned about it," he said, "is because people were mean to me in school."

"I didn't take you for someone who had been bullied." I replied.

"It's not a big deal." He shrugged.

I scooted closer to him, propping my arm up behind his head. He was timid at first, but I could see him melting with every breath he took. He wanted to talk to me, he wanted to confess his secrets and express his emotions, he just needed a little push.

"I was really... outgoing, I guess," he said, "I tried to make friends with anybody and everybody... but no one wanted to be friends with me."

I frowned at him but stayed silent in an attempt to make him keep talking to fill the awkward silence.

"After a while, it started hurting so bad that I just went off by myself," he continued, "but they'd always come back and say stuff."

I bit my lip, trying to think of something to say. He looked sad, much sadder than I had wanted him to.

“I would have hung out with you,” I smiled, “and I wouldn’t have been mean to you.”

He finally made eye contact with me. He seemed to be searching my eyes, trying to discover if I was telling the truth or just trying to make him feel better. After a few silent moments, I slid closer to him and slowly placed my legs over his lap. He instinctively turned his body, angling himself toward me.

Breathing deeply, I placed my hand on his cheek, stroking his skin with my thumb. He raised his hand to cover mine, his skin warm against mine. I wasn’t scared of him like I had been at first, but I wasn’t as confident around him as I had been this morning.

“You can cry if you need to.” I whispered.

It was as if my words had cut right through the walls he had put up. He began to cry, his warm tears falling into my hand. I wiped the tears off his cheeks, then snuggled into him, trying to give him some sort of comfort. He in turn wrapped his arms around my body and hugged me tightly to him.

"Sorry, that was weird." He sniffled as he finished crying.
"You had a rough day... it's not weird to be upset about it." I replied.
"It was weak." He snapped.
"Crying doesn't make you weak," I said, "vulnerability does not make you weak... vulnerability takes strength, Matt."

He looked at me for a few seconds, his brows furrowed. He was tense now, as if he was trying to protect himself.

"I should go shower." He said, shaking his head.

He stood up, effectively pushing me off him. I watched him as he left, wondering if my plan had gone awry.

Chapter Three: Back to Base

Matt's coughing woke me up the next morning. As I blinked awake, I saw that his hair was still damp from his shower, but he was fully clothed and ready for work. I sat up as I watched him cough into his elbow.

"What are you doing?" I asked him.

He turned abruptly, as if he had expected me to still be asleep.

"I'm getting ready for work." He responded.

"The Intergalactic Health Organization's laws clearly state that anyone with symptoms of illness will work from home." I retorted.

"I'm fine." He argued.

I raised an eyebrow at him and crossed my arms over my chest.

"Do you not remember the intergalactic pandemic of the 3000's?" I challenged.

I was not about to drop this issue, and he knew it. Matt looked at me and sighed in exasperation.

"I'll wear a mask, alright?" he huffed.

"You're only going to work if you don't have a fever." I said, rising from the bed.

"I don't, I'm telling you." He rolled his eyes.

I stormed off to the bathroom and began rifling through the cabinets until I found the thermometer. I then marched back out into the bedroom and towards Matt.

"Sit." I commanded.

He rolled his eyes but obeyed my command. I passed the thermometer over his head, and it flashed green. He did not have a fever, much to my chagrin.

"See? I told you. I'll wear a mask." Matt said.

He walked out into living room, and I followed him. He grabbed a black, full-face mask from one of the drawers and pulled it onto his face. He looked ridiculous, but I forced myself not to laugh so he wouldn't get mad and not wear it.

Once he left, I went about my normal day. I had hoped to work out tonight in the gym with Matt, but I knew that he shouldn't go to any public places with his sickness. Though I hadn't told him, I knew exactly what illness had afflicted him. Anyone from Ai'Windel would know, considering it affected nearly every child on Ai'Windel at one point or another.

I felt bad that I had been the carrier for his sickness, but I was more focused on the opportunity this would provide. I knew exactly how to take care of him while he was sick and since I was immune, I could seem like a selfless caretaker for him.

Unfortunately, there was not a decent opportunity for me to care for him that day or the next. He had the early symptoms, which incLuded a sore throat and violent coughing, which I remembered all too well, but he refused to rest or stay home. In fact, it wasn't until the third day, when the symptoms got much worse, that I was able to convince him to stay home, even though he refused to rest.

"You're going to rest for a while after Lunch." I told him, strolling into the office.

"I don't have time." He retorted.

"Make time," I demanded, "I ordered you soup; they're going to leave it outside the door.... so, when you hear me open the door, get your butt in the kitchen."

He growled in frustration at me, his congestion causing it to sound nasally and quite funny. I left him to his work and waited in the living room for the food to be delivered. The door opened and revealed a tray of food on the ground. I picked it up and walked over to the table, where I set the tray down.

"Matt!" I yelled.

I could hear his sniffing as he padded towards the kitchen. He plopped down in the chair opposite me and grabbed the soup from the tray. He sniffed in between bites, filling the silence that would have permeated the room otherwise.

He went back to the office after Lunch, leaving me to amuse myself once more. Despite my attempts every hour, he refused to leave his work. So, I decided that I would just go about my normal day and leave him to it.

It wasn't until the next day that I decided I could not let him continue working anymore. His sneezing and sniffling woke me up and summoned me to the office. He was in the exact same chair he had been in the day before, but he looked much worse.

Matt sniffled as he tried his best to keep working. His eyes watered as he tried to focus. He looked terrible, and I felt terrible for him. I bit my lip, determined to carry out my resoLution.

I walked over to him and removed the tablet from his hands, wishing that of all the treatments the galaxy had made in the past centuries, there had been one effective treatment for these small illnesses. It was too bad that they were seen as trivial sicknesses that needed nothing more than water and rest.

“Come on, we’re going to get you better.” I said, pulling his arm.

“No, I have to keep working.” He argued.

“You have to rest,” I countered, “you have to get better...come on.”

He begrudgingly followed me to the bedroom, where I laid him down. I covered him in blankets, making him look like a small child and not the intimidating Supreme Commander of the Intergalactic Endeavour. I gave him a glass of water and some medicine before sitting opposite him. He grabbed a tissue from the tissue box on the bedside table and blew his nose.

I stood up and crossed over to the bathroom to get a washcloth. I soaked it in warm water, wrung it out, then returned to the bedroom. I sat opposite Matt once more and began patting his face with the warm cloth.

"This always made me feel better when I was sick," I smiled, "it always made me feel cleaner and warmer."

He seemed to be studying my face.

"Why are you doing this?" he asked.

"Doing what, exactly?" I frowned.

"Treating me like this," he said, "treating me like a person."

"Aren't you?" I chuckled.

"Well, yeah...but..." he trailed off.

"But what?" I asked.

"I don't know," he sighed, "I feel like I don't deserve it."

"Matt," I sat down opposite him, "I know you basically kidnapped me, but you've been so sweet to me...this whole time. Let me be sweet to you."

He frowned at my words, which I would admit had been a bit overkill. Still, it seemed that my words had accomplished my purpose. He allowed me to take care of him and he eventually fell into a deep sleep. I used the time to clean up a bit and order the meals for the day.

I woke him up only to bring him food and water. Fortunately, he preferred to be left alone for a majority of the day to rest, so I had time to go about my regular routine. The only change was that I ate my meals in the bedroom with Matt.

"Why are you doing this, really?" Matt asked over dinner, "why are you taking such good care of me?"

"Look, Matt, I know we don't know each other well... or at all, really," I said, "but I'm still worried about you. You shouldn't be alone right now."

"Technically, I should," he retorted, "you're risking your own health taking care of me."

I only smiled in response and began cleaning up. He watched me carefully, but I ignored him and closed the door. I ended up sleeping on the couch in the living room so I wouldn't disturb his sleep but would still be close if he needed something. I wasn't sure if he knew I had done so, but it didn't really matter that much to me; I had done it and that was all that mattered.

The next morning, he was doing much better, so I allowed him to get up to shower. I did not, however, allow him to do work of any sort. I brought him his meals and fetched anything else he might need, in addition to entertaining him with small talk.

"Why don't you have a lover?" he asked, "surely *you* have enough time to find one."

"While I resent your insinuation, I admit that is true," I sighed, "but I don't know if I really want a lover. A supreme enemy you can make out with sometimes in secret sounds a lot more interesting, don't you think?"

I smiled maliciously as he bLushed and sat up. My words had the effect I wanted on him, and he had nowhere to run now.

"Can I have some more tissues?" he asked awkwardly.

I nodded and stood up to retrieve what he'd asked for. He avoided any further conversation for the remainder of the day, pretending to be fixated on whatever holoprojection he was watching. I slept on the couch once more, since he was still quite ill, Lulled to sleep by the faint holoprojection noise coming from the bedroom.

When I woke up the next morning to check on Matt, I found that he had disappeared. After a few moments of looking around, I realized that the shower water was running and that he had probably woken up early and decided to shower while I was still sleeping.

This would be his sixth day of sickness, which most likely meant that he was feeling better. If my experience with the sickness was any indication, he'd probably be feeling more energetic today, but would easily tire. I resolved to allow him to work if he wished, but still care for him as much as he needed and encourage him to rest.

"Good morning." He chirped as he entered the kitchen.

"You look better." I noted.

"I feel better." He grinned.

He sat down at the table and began shoveling food into his mouth. He hadn't eaten very much in the past few days, so I wasn't surprised that he was so hungry. Still, there was something comical about watching him eat his food as if it was going to disappear at any moment.

"You should still work from here until you're not contagious anymore." I said.

"I'm working from here until we're back on base," he replied, "the Intergalactic Endeavour is very serious about the health and safety of its' members. Now that they've figured out I'm sick, I have to stay here."

"And when will we be back on base?" I inquired.

"Four days... on Japris 14th." He replied.

"Japris 14th?" I echoed, "I can't believe it's been nearly two weeks since I got here."

"It's gone by quickly." He agreed.

It truly had gone by quickly. If someone would have asked me, I would have guessed that I had been with him a week. How was it that I had ignored the dates on the electronics that Matt had given me? Had I really been that preoccupied during my time here?

Matt continued to improve as the days went by, and he began to join me in my daily at-home workouts. He was much stronger and better than me, but I tried not to get too competitive. After all, I wasn't doing the workouts to compete, but to stay strong for any unprecedented future trials I might face. If there was one thing I had learned from this situation it was that I needed to be prepared for anything and everything.

"We're back on base tomorrow," Matt said as he slipped into bed next to me, "are you ready?"

"I guess." I sighed.

"You'll be with me the entire time," he told me, "So don't worry about it too much."

"What do I have to do once we're back?" I inquired.

"Same thing you do here... except you'll have more space." He answered.

He wrapped his arm around my waist and scooted closer to me.

"You'll have a private gym... and your own bedroom if you want it." He said.

I stared into his brown eyes, which were searching my face for any sign of my answer.

"I don't know," I sighed, "I think I'm just too used to sleeping next to someone now."

He tried to hide it, but I could tell that he was pleased. Even though my answer was mostly for his benefit, seeing his reaction made me happy.

"Come here." He chuckled.

He pulled me closer, and I turned my back to him. I hadn't lied that I was used to sleeping next to someone now, and I wouldn't be lying if I had said that I had come to enjoy sleeping next to someone. In fact, I wouldn't be lying if I said that I had come to enjoy sleeping next to Matticas Damiran.

"Astraella, Astraella." Matt whispered as he gently shook me awake.

I blinked my eyes as I tried to focus on his face.

"You need to get up if you want to get dressed before they take your stuff." He said.

I nodded and pushed myself up into a sitting position. Matt left the room, presumably to get his own things. Meanwhile, I stumbled towards my racks of clothing, which I had only recently moved into Matt's closet. It wasn't an ideal situation, but it was better than them crowding up the living area.

I didn't want to dress too fancily for the occasion, but I also didn't want to offend Matt or the Intergalactic Endeavour by dressing too casually. I finally decided on a loose-fitting dress that was the color of the night sky, with jeweled stars embroidered onto it. I pulled my blonde curls into a loose bun, pulling out tendrils of hair to frame my face and make me look more attractive.

Matt was already ready and waiting for me when I entered the living room. He looked taller and more regal than usual. I began wondering if I was underdressed for the occasion.

"Are you ready?" he asked, reaching his hand out.

I nodded and took his hand, trying to ready myself for whatever might happen.

"Just stay with me," he said, "we'll have to walk past the other members of the Intergalactic Endeavour, but we'll go straight to my penthouse."

"Penthouse... fancy." I chuckled.

"You'll like it better than here, I'm sure." He smiled.

I smiled in response as the door opened before us. He led me outside and down the empty halls. The beautiful vastness of space was no longer outside the window, but was replaced by tall, spiraled buildings, mountains, and an extensive body of water.

"We'll walk off the landing pad past the ship's crew," he whispered as we walked, "then we'll go through the private tunnel down the base ramp... more people will be there."

"More?" I frowned.

"Intergalactic Endeavour members and supporters who have long awaited my return." He responded.

My eyes widened and my heart began to beat quicker as I imagined how many eyes would be on me.

"We'll get straight in the car from there," he said, "and go right to the base."

"You said before that we would be going straight to the base off the ship." I frowned.

"We will... pretty much." He shrugged.

I scoffed in response. We finally arrived at the ship's main door, which opened slowly before us. Two lines of people, one on either side of the walkway, greeted us outside. They all watched us solemnly, lowering their gaze as we walked by. I could feel their stare return to our retreating figures as soon as they were out of our line of sight.

Matt pulled me along towards a tunnel that was covered with grass and plants. The tunnel was cool and dark, ilLuminated by small bulbs in the ceiling. It let out at a ridged ramp, which I guessed was supposed to look like steps; I treated them as such as I stepped carefully behind Matt.

I had half expected the crowd before us to applaud, but they merely stared at us with great focus and interest; the walk down felt more like a death march than a welcoming celebration. A few people were taking photos of us, but most just gawked at us as we entered the car waiting for us.

"They're not happy about me being here?" I meant it as a question, but it was more like a statement.

"It's always like this." He shrugged.

"That's... fun." I murmured.

We drove past huge, circular buildings which were surrounded by crowds. The car slowly made its way towards another tunnel, the top of which was glass. The tunnel let out at a long, winding bridge. The car drove slowly on this bridge, despite the fact that there were no people around. As we came to an intersection, I understood why.

There was a scanner just before the intersection and a laser bridge that barred the road straight ahead. A look to the right informed me that the other road led straight back to the city, presumably for the cars which the scanner rejected. As I had suspected, the scanner flashed green and the laser bridge disappeared in front of us, allowing us passage down the alabaster road.

"No one's allowed here except for members of the Intergalactic Endeavour," Matt told me, "So, there won't be any more crowds."

"Thank God." I said, more to myself than to him.

We exited the car, and I looked around me. The base's building encircled us, closing us off from the rest of the people on the planet. It was grey, cold, and foreboding. I shivered as I studied it.

"Come on." Matt grabbed my hand and pulled me along.

We entered the massive building at a faster pace than I was comfortable with. I hadn't had time to count how many floors there were, but I knew there were probably about 10. I saw as we entered the elevator that I had been correct. Once we exited the elevator, we walked through the circular halls to yet another elevator.

"How many floors are there?!" I finally asked.

"Ten for everyone else... eleven for us." He winked.

Matt placed his hand on the scanner and the elevator opened. He entered first and I stepped in hesitantly behind him. The elevator lifted us up to the highest floor on the base.

As the doors opened, Matt stepped out. I followed him, looking around at the grey room surrounding us. It was clean and formal, a very fitting room for the Supreme Commander of the Intergalactic Endeavour.

"I'll give you a tour tomorrow," he said, "right now, we need to get ready for the Return Ball."

"The Return Ball?!" I exclaimed, "you said no more crowds!"

"It's not a crowd... just all the members of the Intergalactic Endeavour." He replied.

I scoffed and rolled my eyes at him. I had *not* signed up for this much attention and social interaction.

"Hey, you work for *me* now, remember?" he snapped, approaching me in a malicious manner.

I blinked up at him, wondering where this outburst had come from. He had been fairly nice to me this entire time, which I supposed I should be grateful for, but my understanding was that he was going to continue being kind to me. Though he had only said one sentence, I felt more trapped in that moment than I had ever felt in my time here.

"I offered you a job and you told the soldiers you would take it," he hissed, "if you don't want to work for me, for the Intergalactic Endeavour, then I suppose we'll just have to go back to Ai'Windel."
"I'll go to the ball with you, if that's what you want." I said, my throat tight.

I wasn't a particularly brave person, especially since I had never had an opportunity to build any sort of bravery. I had high ambitions for myself, and I wanted to believe that I would laugh in the face of danger, but I really didn't know if I could do it. Now that I was faced with the possibility of my planet and my family being attacked once more, I realized that I wasn't very brave at all.

Matt seemed pleased at my answer, but I was shaken by his sudden outburst. My throat felt sore, and my body felt weak. I was going to crack under the stress at any moment.

"Is there a bathroom? I need to freshen up." I squeaked.

"Right over there." He pointed to my left.

I walked in the direction that he had pointed and closed myself in the bathroom. My body shook as tears fell from my eyes. I wasn't just shaken by his outburst, but I was also disappointed that I wasn't getting as far with him as I thought. I was deLusional to think that he actually cared about me as a person. No, he just thought of me as some little employee he could order around.

"Astraella?" Matt called as he knocked on the door.

I wiped the tears from my eyes and cleared my throat.

"Yeah?" I returned.

"Your dresses are here for you to try on... when you're ready." He said.

He sounded so sweet now, just as he usually did. How did he do that? How could he be so nice and sweet but then lash out at me like that? Did he have some sort of anger management issue? Or was he just tired and cranky?

"My dresses?" I asked.

"For the ball." He said.

It all finally clicked for me, and the tightness in my throat disappeared. I chuckled to myself as my eyes started to dry.

"Just a minute." I said.

I could hear his footsteps retreating from the door. I splashed some cold water on my face, smiled at myself in the mirror, and exited the room. Matt was waiting for me near the elevator, in what I could now see was the main living room of his penthouse. There was a rack of long evening gowns next to him, waiting for and tempting me.

"You ordered me dresses for the ball?" I inquired nonchalantly.

"I sent the dressmakers here your measurements when I ordered your other clothes," he answered, "and some guidelines of what I thought would be appropriate."

"And you got my measurements how?" I asked.

"From the scan." He said.

I sifted through the dresses, trying to hide the smirk I knew was playing on my lips. No wonder he'd been so upset when I expressed my displeasure at accompanying him to the ball; he'd been planning on showing me off there for weeks. He had probably been excitedly plotting this night since he'd received my scan.

"Try them on, I want to see how they look." Matt said, collapsing into one of the pLush couches.

I grabbed the first dress on the rack, even though I knew it wouldn't be the right one. It was a terribly gaudy dress made of some sort of greenish yellow, shiny fabric. The sleeves stopped just before my wrists and the skirt ended just below my knees. Although the dress hugged my body well, as it should since it was made to my measurements, it made me look short and awkward.

Matt furrowed his brows as soon as he saw me. It was almost humorous how hard he was trying not to say anything mean to me. I merely laughed at his expression and carried off the next dress, a gold, shiny dress that was not nearly as ugly as its predecessor.

This dress had only one sleeve and made me look reminiscent of a Greek goddess. The skirt was cut shorter in the front and dragged behind me in the back. It fit me well and looked rather good, but I wasn't entirely sure that this was the perfect one.

"What do you think?" I asked Matt.

"It's much better than the last," he replied, "but I think you should try on the other two just in case."

I shrugged in agreement and grabbed the next dress. Unlike the other dresses, this one was black and matte. There were two knotted straps and a pLunging neckline which was accentuated by dark jewels running down the front. Even though it was loose, it fit me nicely, and I thought it would definitely be a contender.

"This one?" I twirled into the room.

"I don't know..." he furrowed his brows, "I liked the other one better."

"Well, I'll try the last one," I said, "and then I'll change back into that one if you don't like it."

Inside my makeshift dressing room, I got a good look at the last dress that Matt had gotten for me. It was silver and sparkly, with thin straps and crossed bands down the bodice. I put it on and noted with some uneasiness that the neckline was much lower than what I was used to, but not lower than the one on the previous dress. Not to mention the fact that the dress was skintight on me, excepting the bottom half of the skirt portion.

I emerged from the bathroom feeling slightly uncomfortable but also oddly confident. Matt looked me over as I appeared in front of him, one eyebrow slightly raised as he did so. Okay, maybe I actually did look as nice as I thought.

"You look good in that dress." He complimented.

"Thanks." I mumbled shyly.

He looked me over again, a smile playing on his lips.

"Let's eat Lunch and then we can get ready together." He said softly.

I nodded and headed back to the bathroom to change. Lunch was rather awkward and stiff, but I didn't mind. I needed time to think about Matt and about the situation I was in. He was certainly giving me mixed signals and I didn't know which ones to believe, if I was supposed to believe any of them at all. He wasn't terribly easy to read, except in his more vulnerable states.

After Lunch, Matt showed me where the two bedrooms were. He went to his bedroom to prepare for the ball, while I made use of the extra bedroom. I noted as I got dressed how flattering the dress actually was. It was a perfect fit, and it made me look more beautiful than I ever had.

I emerged from the room well after Matt was done. He was waiting outside his bedroom for me, his arms crossed as he leaned against the wall. He looked me over once more but squinted at my hair.

"What's wrong?" I asked, shifting uncomfortably.

"Your hair... you should pull it back." He noted.

"Oh... uh..." I stammered.

I had tried to make my hair look decent, but I didn't really have the tools to do so. Had I brought my things from Ai'Windel, he might have approved of my hair.

"You'll be able to see your face and the dress better." He added.

"I don't really have anything to pull my hair back with." I chuckled nervously.

Matt motioned for me to follow him and walked towards the main room. He picked up a box beneath the rack of dresses and shifted through the items inside.

"Sit down, I'll do it for you." He commanded.

I did as he said, trusting my long, blonde locks to his care. I could feel his touch as he twisted my hair back, his smooth skin brushing against my face. His touch was gentle, delicate, skillfully curling my hair out of my face.

"Go see if you like it." He said.

I stood up and stepped towards the bathroom, my heart beating quickly with anticipation. I saw in the mirror that my hair had been twisted back out of my face and pinned with silver star hair clips, which matched my dress perfectly. I looked beautiful, like an angel. I walked back out to the main room and nodded in approval to Matt.

"Come on, let's go." He said, wrapping his arm around my waist.

His hands seemed to slide up and down my body as we walked, making me wonder if he was doing it on purpose or accidentally. We took the first elevator down to the 10th floor, and then took the other elevator down to the third floor. Matt kept a tight grip on me, and I could have sworn he pulled me closer every time we passed by someone else.

"Tell me about this whole... ball situation." I said as the elevator traveled downwards.

"The social room opens at 1500, we'll probably be the first ones there," he told me, "Most people will get there within the hour, and then at 1700 we'll all have dinner."

"And then?" I pressed.

"We'll all dance and talk the night away." He sighed.

I rolled my eyes just as the elevator doors began to open. Matt pushed me forward, leading me towards the ballroom from behind. There were a few people inside the room, all of whom stopped their conversations to look at us. They all made polite nods to Matt and looked at me with intense curiosity.

"They're all staring at me." I whispered through gritted teeth.

"Why shouldn't they? You're new," he chuckled, "not to mention, you look gorgeous in that dress."

"Yeah, thanks." I snorted.

A short, dark-haired woman approached us. She smiled, but her almond-shaped eyes were cold and menacing.

"Supreme Commander Damiran," she drawled, "how lovely to see you again."

"Thank you, Miss Lu." He responded.

I noticed with some displeasure that since Miss Diu was wearing heeled shoes, we two were the same height and could easily look into each other's eyes.

"Is this my replacement?" she asked mockingly.

I took a deep breath as I stared at the curvaceous woman before me, my eyes narrowing.

"She's not here to be my assistant," Matt answered, "She's my companion."

So many emotions flashed on her face in such a little amount of time that I was unable to analyze them. She was soon back to her blasé expression, which infuriated me. I wrapped my arm around Matt's torso in an attempt to throw her once more. She glanced down at my arm for a moment, a peeved look passing briefly over her face. I definitely would not get along with this hateful woman.

"Companion?" she snorted, "what an... interesting title."

She smirked and I clenched my arm in response. As if sensing my discontent, Matt pulled me closer and began moving his hand slowly up and down my torso. The motion fulfilled its purpose of pacifying the rage burning inside of me.

"It's a unique one, to be sure," Matt said, "but she essentially has all the rights and powers of a high-ranking officer."

"Hmm." Miss Diu hummed.

"Excuse us." Matt replied, pulling me with him.

A man with a tray full of champagne glasses paused by Matt. He grabbed a glass and turned to me.

"Do you want some?" he asked.

I nodded fervently in response, my cheeks burning. He handed me the glass he held and grabbed another. I placed the glass to my lips and tilted the liquid into my mouth; the burn of the alcohol distracted me from my anger. As the man with the tray continued on his way, we were approached by three people, dressed in golds and blacks. The oldest-looking woman approached us first. I noted to myself that she was my height, gaunt, with ebony hair and eyes.

"Supreme Commander," her pale lips barely moved as she spoke, "I cannot tell you how pleased I am that you have returned."

"General Porter," Matt smiled, "I am pleased to be back."

The last two in the group appeared at General Porter's side. On her left was a blonde man, just slightly shorter than I. On her right was a brunette woman with a wise and motherly face.

“Astraella, I’d like to introduce you to General Uxe, General Porter, and Brigadier Tenn.” Matt said, motioning to each individual.

“I’m very pleased to meet you all.” I smiled.

“Pleased to meet you, too... Astraella, is it?” Brigadier Tenn replied.

“She’s my new companion.” Matt added.

Their faces all seemed to brighten at the word.

“A Companion?” General Porter exclaimed.

“You’ve finally found one, eh?” General Uxe chuckled.

Porter and Tenn shot the man a reproachful look. Uxe looked down at his feet in response. Though I wasn’t pleased that General Uxe’s comment had made Matt stiffen in response, I was grateful that he had inadvertently provided me with a new piece of information on Matt.

"It's so lovely that we finally have a Companion here," Tenn grinned, "someone to help our Supreme Commander in this troubling time."

"I hope I am up to the task." I chuckled nervously.

"She underestimates herself," Matt said, "I think she'll prove to be more than worthy."

The conversation continued from there, becoming more casual. I soon found myself chatting and laughing with them as if we were old friends. I felt comfortable and confident with Matt by my side, even though he frightened me sometimes with his grand and commanding demeanor.

Dinner was announced not long after we had started talking and we all made our way into the dining room. I was seated at Matt's right, next to General Uxe and across from General Porter. Brigadier Tenn sat next to General Porter, completing our original quintet from earlier. We continued our conversation as we ate and were eventually joined by others.

I met many of the other high-ranking officers that night, though I had trouble remembering their names. All I knew was that there was a total of ten generals, including Porter and Uxe, twenty brigadiers, the best of which was Tenn, fifty colonels, and a hundred battalion leaders. They were not all at our table of course, but I was made aware of them throughout the conversation.

"What will we do, now?" I asked Matt as soon as the dining room was clear of others.

"We all usually go back into the social room for conversation and dancing." He told me.

Matt offered me his arm and I accepted it. He took me back into the ballroom and I found myself counting the people inside. There was no way that all of the higher-ups were in this room, but at least I knew how many there were now. If I made it out of here alive, the information would be incredibly valuable.

"Do you want to dance?" Matt whispered to me, pulling me out of my thoughts.

"Sure." I shrugged.

We spun around the dance floor, past other couples doing the exact same thing. As we danced, I found myself trying to do the math. If there were a hundred battalion leaders, that meant that there were a hundred battalions, each consisting of 1,000 troops. That meant that were at least 100,000 troops, not to mention the higher-ranking officers. In fact, I hadn't even accounted for the supplementary soldiers.

"What are you thinking about?" Matt asked.

"Just... everything." I shrugged.

He raised an eyebrow at me, enticing me to say more.

"Things are so different here," I said, "different from the ship, different from my planet..."

I sighed and looked around us. I had said that as a distraction from what I had actually been thinking, but it was true. In Ai'Windel, everyone was casual and natural and free. Here, everything seemed cold and stiff and foreign.

"Do you regret coming with me?" he inquired softly.

I looked up at him and noticed a hint of sadness in his eyes. My hypothesis from earlier was right; he needed me now and he was scared to lose me. He needed me to accompany him to things like this, to make him feel loved and needed.

"I don't." I smiled, deciding that it was best to boost his ego.

We were among the last people to leave the ball that night. I took my shoes off as we walked towards the first elevator, letting them swing at my side as we walked. As soon as we were back, I went to the extra bedroom to change into more comfortable clothing before shuffling back to Matt's bedroom to collapse on his immense bed.

I closed my eyes, relaxing into the plush softness of the bed. Matt emerged from his bathroom not long after, freshly showered and ready to sleep. He chuckled at me, somehow sprawled across his massive bed despite my relative smallness. He gently moved me to the other side, probably thinking that I was already asleep. I kept my eyes closed as he turned off the lights and climbed into bed next to me.

"I think... I think I might be falling in love with you." He whispered in my ear.

It took everything in me not to open my eyes. Had he really just said that? Was I imagining things? He sighed deeply and wrapped his arm around my waist, assuming his usual position next to me.

"You're so warm." He hummed.

Okay, well, maybe it hadn't been my imagination... maybe he was just very, very drunk.

Chapter Four: Feelings, Feelings

It had been three months since Matt had confessed his feelings to me while he thought I was asleep. I had thought that he was just incredibly drunk... but the way he had been acting recently told me otherwise. He'd taken me around the base and around the planet, using the excuse that he wanted me to be familiar with my new home. He'd also started listening more attentively when I talked and staring at me when he thought I wouldn't notice. If he wasn't falling in love with me, then I truly didn't know what was wrong with him.

I had been thinking about confronting him all week, I just couldn't think of a way to do it. I didn't want to ruin the moments he was creating. Still, his confession was gnawing at me, and I knew sooner or later I'd have to face him. He entered the room as I thought through this, startling me from my train of thought.

"Matt." I said.

"Astra." He smiled.

"We need to talk." I replied.

Matt frowned at me, his eyes questioning.

"About?" he asked.

"Sit down." I commanded.

Hesitantly, he acquiesced to my wishes. I tried to distance myself from him, so my head would remain clear and not be clouded by my nerves.

"The night after the ball..." I began.

He didn't seem nervous... had I dreamt his confession? Was I just imagining his actions from the past week?

"I heard what you said to me." I blurted out.

I knew that I had to stop questioning myself and just confess.

"What did I say?" he asked.

He seemed more nervous now; perhaps I hadn't dreamt it.

"You said you're falling in love with me." I said.

He blinked at me a few times, then chuckled dryly and shook his head.

"You were very unconscious after the ball," he retorted, "how would you even remember something like that?"

"I know what I heard." I argued.

He scoffed and stood up, stepping slowly across the room. He was obviously in denial, but his words and actions made me surer of what I'd heard.

"It's okay." I murmured.

My words, which were meant to be reassuring, seemed to set him off. He stormed off to his bedroom and slammed the door. I sat there for a while, trying to process what had just transpired between us.

Matt did not leave his room the entire night, at least not to my knowledge. I ended up sleeping in the extra room, feeling rather cold and lonely. My thoughts were a cyclone in my mind, keeping me awake for a majority of the night.

When I exited the bedroom the next morning, Matt was sitting on the couch in the main living room. He was fully dressed and sat up straight, as if he had been waiting for me for hours. There seemed to be no emotions in his entire body, just ice.

"Good morning." I said hesitantly.

Matt turned towards me, his eyes piercing into mine.

"Your time here is done," he said, "I'm sending you back to your home planet."

He turned from me and began tapping on his holopad. His coldness infuriated me just as much as his words had.

"My time here is done when *I* say it's done." I retorted.

He didn't answer, so I walked around to the other side of him. I bent down on my knees and placed my arms on his thighs. I stared at him, trying to get him to look back at me.

"You are breaking down the Intergalactic Endeavour." Matt said.

"I'm breaking down *you,"* I argued, "and you're scared."

He looked up at me, his eyes cold and callous.

"You don't want to do this," I told him, "You don't want to lose me."

"Exactly." He said, standing.

I pushed myself off the floor, feeling feeble in my position so far below him.

“I’m not going to leave you.” I stated.

Matt’s hand flew up to my neck, startling me so much that I almost lost my balance. His grip was not tight, it was simply a show of the power that he had over me. He wanted to show me that he was in control here, but I knew the truth.

“I’m not going to leave you,” I repeated, “because I feel the same way about you.”

His face softened and so did his grip. His hand rested on my collarbone now and I knew he could feel my quickened heartbeat. It was working, just as I hoped it would.

“Arrangements have already been made,” he told me, “You leave tomorrow morning.”

Matt exited the penthouse via the elevator, leaving me alone and utterly confused. We had never even been in a relationship and yet I felt as though we had just broken things off. Slowly, the pain turned to anger, and I decided it was time to do what I had truly come to do.

I stormed off to the extra bedroom, my bedroom, where I had hidden my things from Ai'Windel. I had laid the blue dress I had worn that day, the dress that I had picked out years ago just in case the Intergalactic Endeavour came to visit. After moving the dress off of the white linen boots I had worn with it that fateful day, I reached into the hardy boots, searching for the piece of paper I had carried with me the past weeks.

The names of my family members were etched on it in black ink. I had done it shortly after I had arrived here, when my motivations were starting to dissolve in favor of my emotions. I read their names aloud, just as I did every day that I was alone.

“Rylen Wander, Tarin Wander, Marsa Wander,” I whispered, “Olver Wander, Sofi Wander.”

I looked straight ahead, lost in thought. I needed to enact my plan, sooner rather than later. I folded the paper and shoved it back into my boot. I stood up, my eyes not leaving the blank wall in front of me as they filled with tears.

“I’m going to take over the Intergalactic Endeavour for all of you,” I said to the wall, pretending my family was there with me, “just as I’ve promised you I would all these years.”

I had to do this for them and for everyone else in the galaxy who suffered because of the Intergalactic Endeavour. I had to be covert, I had to be careful, for them. If I was caught, my family would lose everything, including their lives. At this point, I was sure that Matt would do a lot worse to a lot more people if I was caught.

Chapter Five: The Plan

Once my emotions had stopped clouding my judgement, I came to the realization that Matt never had any true feelings for me. He liked what I provided him: an ego boost, comfort, friendship, and warmth at night. This realization provided me even more motivation to carry out my plan.

Meals were delivered for me, but Matt did not return until well after dinner. He was silent and went straight to his bedroom, not even sparing me a glance. The anger bubbled up in me once more, but I knew I had to keep a cool head if things were going to work out the way I wanted them to. I couldn't move now; I'd have to wait until a majority of the members of the Intergalactic Endeavour were asleep. More importantly, I needed to wait until Supreme Commander Matticas Damiran was asleep.

It had been nearly four months since I had met Matt and, in that time, I had learned almost everything about him. I knew all of his routines and I knew how to tell when he was asleep. In fact, I didn't just know when he was asleep; I knew when he was so deeply asleep that next to nothing could wake him.

Anyone who heard our story would probably think that Matt was the villain and that I was the helpless, captive princess. There was more than met the eye, though. I had been planning for a situation like this my entire life. True, everything had worked out much better than I had planned, but to some extent, this situation was all planned by me. I was going to work my way up the ranks of the Intergalactic Endeavour, seduce the Supreme Commander, and take over the organization for myself. Then everyone would see that the helpless, captive princess had truly been the villain of the story all along.

It would be a lie to say that everything had been fake. I could honestly say that everything was carefully planned and had been fake at first, but it wasn't anymore. However, Matt had refused to confess any feelings for me, which meant that I had to go through with the resolution I had made yesterday: get him to say he loved me or follow through with my original plan to take over the Intergalactic Endeavour.

My parents had heard me talking about my plan for half of my life, but they had never thought I could do it, especially not from the inside. Truthfully, I hadn't exactly expected to be picked as the companion of the Supreme Commander right off the bat, but I knew I would get up to the higher ranks somehow. Now that I was here, at the top of the chain, I had to do what I came here for.

I rifled through my closet, looking for the shoebox which contained everything I had gathered over the past few months. There was personal information from Matt, tape with his fingerprints and handprints, photographs of him, and most importantly, information on the base. I put everything in my bag and waited until the lights in the hallway powered down, alerting me that Matt had not been moving around for at least the past hour.

I snuck out of my bedroom and then out the front door. As I walked, I realized how lucky I was to have been given this opportunity. The guards all knew me well, so they did not make a fuss about me going out. In fact, I was able to get to Matt's office with no resistance whatsoever.

I scanned into the office with Matt's fingerprints, holding my breath as I did so. The lock eventually beeped, and I sighed in relief. The door opened for me, and I stepped inside, looking around to make sure no one was watching.

As far as I knew, Matt didn't get alerts when someone else entered his office, because only he was authorized to do so, but I still had to work quickly. I crossed over to his desk and unlocked his holocomputer using both his thumbprint and password that I had deduced from the information I had received from him. Just as I was about to open his email and documents to begin my work, his background caught my eye.

His background, to my complete surprise, was a picture of him and me at the first Intergalactic Endeavour ball he had taken me to. His arm was wrapped around me, his hand firmly cupping the upper portion of my ribcage as he kept me securely pressed against him. I was holding a glass in my hand and laughing or smiling at something, and he was looking down at me with the most enamored look I had ever seen.

"Stop it Astra," I whispered to myself, "he told you he doesn't feel anything for you, now get back to work."

Had I not said this to myself, I may not have been able to focus on the task at hand. I continued working, but I couldn't shake my thoughts. Why would he have a picture of us as his holocomputer background if he didn't at least like me? In fact, why would he have a picture of us as his background if he didn't love me? Hell, I didn't even have him in my background pictures. And why would he have said anything to me that night? Surely, he wasn't *that* drunk.

Everything would have been much easier if Matt would have just fallen for me. I could have used my power over him to convince him to name me Supreme Commandress of the Intergalactic Endeavour, then taken it over that way. Now, all I could do was download his files, analyze the data, then use it against him.

My holodrive beeped and flashed green, alerting me that the files were downloaded. I removed the drive from Matt's holocomputer and stuffed it into my pocket. After turning everything off and looking around to make sure no one was watching, I exited Matt's office and hurried back to his penthouse.

As I laid in my bed that night, I ran through my plan over and over again. What little sleep I got was plagued with nightmares about it not working. When the light streamed in from my window the next morning, I was feeling exhausted and desperate. I had stressed myself out so much, that I became ill the second I got up. Since my original plan had required my work to start well before Matt awoke, I had to settle for waiting until I was done being sick. When I eventually felt better, I resolved that I still had sufficient time to enact a backup plan.

I ate breakfast as quickly as I could, got dressed and ready, then hurried out of the penthouse towards Matt's office. I walked past the shiny, white desk in the lobby, which was now illuminated in the harsh overhead lighting. Behind the desk was Miss Diu, her dark and narrow eyes boring holes in my head.

Her malevolence had not bothered me in the past month or so, because after Matt's confession I knew I had an advantage over her. Not only was the Supreme Commander allowing me to live with him, but he was also falling for me, or so I had thought before yesterday. Still, I knew I was more attractive than her, especially to Matt, and my anger was making me want to gloat.

With an evil smirk, I sauntered over to Miss Diu's desk. She smiled at me in an almost mocking way, as if she knew that Matt was sending me home. I leaned across the desk, trying to project an air of confidence and indifference. I could not under any circumstances let my rival know that I was bothered about the situation in any way.

"Miss Diu, would you mind pointing me to Matt's office?" I put the emphasis on his name.

"Shouldn't you be packing your bags?" she shot back.

I only laughed and shifted my gaze to a waterfall to the right of her. I couldn't let her words wound me, not now.

"That's not going to be necessary," I smiled, "now, where's Matt's office?"

She glared at me again and clenched her jaw.

"Right... straight down the hall." She answered stiffly.

I knew where his office was, of course, but I couldn't let anyone know that. Asking for directions was the perfect way to shift all suspicion off me, aggravating Sara Diu was only an added bonus. I strutted dramatically towards Matt's office, trying to infuriate Sara even more. I knocked on his door and waited for him to allow me in.

"Astraella?" he frowned, "how did you get here?"
"I asked your assistant at the front desk." I replied.

He nodded in understanding, and I silently thanked God that I had the good sense to do such a thing. If he knew that I had been here before, he would definitely be suspicious.

"She was super weird to me, by the way." I noted, trying to change the subject.

I needed to keep things light and casual if I had any chance of staying here. Tension was already permeating the air between us, slowly convincing me to abandon hope.

"She's probably jealous." He shrugged.

"Oh?" I laughed, "and why is that?"

"I used to sleep with her, on occasion." He responded nonchalantly.

I blinked at him. Was he trying to push me away or draw me in? I decided to assume that it was the latter and play along. After all, if I wanted to stay here, I would have to do that anyways.

"You... what now?" I choked.

"You've no right to tell me off about it," he said, "you were not my girlfriend, you were just my companion. You were only an employee of mine."

He paused and looked up at me.

"Besides, it was before you were here." He added quietly.

"Apparently you're very friendly with your employees." I scoffed.

"What's that supposed to mean?" he asked.

I was worried that I had angered him but was comforted by the fact that I was risking very little, since I was still, as far as I knew, scheduled to be sent away.

"You slept with your personal assistant, which is *so wrong* by the way," I said, "and you hired me to keep you company."

"You sound jealous now." He noted.

"I'm not jealous," I laughed, moving closer, "I don't need to be."

This was my last chance to force him to face his feelings for me. I had to show him that even if he wanted to deny it, he wanted me there, with him. I had to use every ounce of charm I had to seduce him into my power.

"Oh?" he responded.

"I know you prefer me to other women," I breathed, "and I know you're under my power more than you'd like to admit."

"Am I now?" he chortled.

I moved closer to him, so that our faces were only inches apart. He held his breath and looked down at me. There was no way he was going to send me away now... I knew it.

"Do you want to kiss me?" I asked, trying to contain my smile.

I laughed and moved away from him when he didn't respond. I had him under my control, whether he knew it or not.

"I'll see you... *tonight*." I called back to him.

I grinned in spite of myself as I made my way back up to the penthouse. When no one came to collect my things that morning, I knew that I had won. I had suspected, or at least hoped, that he loved me and was under my power, but this confirmation felt like such a victory.

Matt entered the penthouse around lunchtime, which was rather unusual for him. I had planned to tease him incessantly when he arrived, but my plans changed as soon as I saw him. He stormed into the main living room, looking angrier than I had ever seen him. I had no clue what was going on, but I knew that two could play at this game. I stood and crossed over to him, my brows furrowed, and my arms folded over my chest.

"What?" I asked.

Before I could draw in another breath, Matt placed his hands on my shoulders and nearly slammed me back into the wall. I gasped in response, trying to comprehend what had just happened. Had he actually intended for me to leave? Was I mistaken in thinking that just because no one came to collect me that I would be allowed to stay?

"You think I'm under your power," he whispered, "but I think the truth is that you're under *my* power."

"Oh?" I breathed.

I felt like I couldn't get a deep enough breath. It felt as if something was blocking my airways, causing me to breathe heavily under his grasp.

"You think I don't see you watching me?" he asked, "you think I don't notice how you snuggle into me at night?"

I didn't respond, because I had no idea how to. If I made the excuse that I was gathering intel or making sure he was still next to me and not rifling through my things, my intentions would be revealed. Other than that, there was truly no justification I could give to him.

"And the worst part is," he smiled maliciously, "you don't try to hide it. You're not even trying to hide it now."

"Now?" I replied breathlessly.

He leaned closer to me, his smile seeming to become more and more malicious the closer he got.

"You're trembling, you're hardly breathing,," he whispered in a gruff voice, "you can't take your eyes off of me...and you're not stopping me."

Before I could protest, his lips were on mine. I had begun to raise my hands to push him off, but I couldn't find the resolve to do so now. I surrendered to my emotions, let him kiss me, and enjoyed every second of it. I didn't even care that I enjoyed it, that I had proved him right. I also didn't care that this was *not* an ideal first kiss.

"I love you." I said once he broke the kiss.

"Do you want me to kiss you again?" he smirked.

"I literally just confessed my love to you, and you ask me that?!" I exclaimed.

"Just answer the question." He returned.

"Yes, of course I want you to kiss me, stupid." I rolled my eyes.

He kissed me again, quickly.

"I love you too," he winked, "I just wanted you to ask me to kiss you again."

"Technically, I didn't ask," I argued, "also, you're a huge jerk."

"A huge jerk that you're in love with." He replied.

This was *definitely* not the ideal situation. My plans never involved actually falling in love with the Supreme Commander of the Intergalactic Endeavour, and now I had to rethink everything. There was no way my original plan could be enacted now.

Chapter Six: Failure

We'd been together, really together, for over a week now, and things seemed to be getting better for us. However, I still hadn't told him about what I had planned to do and what I still might do if given the chance, and that was putting a strain on our relationship. I knew I'd have to confess soon, but everything was going so well for us; it was tempting to just push my secrets down and ignore them for the sake of my temporary happiness.

Today was one of those sublime days I had recently been experiencing. I had woken with the sun, but I did not move from my spot, enjoying the feeling of Matt's arm around me. As much as I wanted to get up and prepare to make the confession that I knew I must make, I could not find the strength to do so. The worst part was that as soon as I resolved to get up and made a move, Matt pulled me back.

"No, please don't get up," he grumbled, "you're my prisoner for the day."

"For the day?" I chuckled, "have I not been for the past few months?"

"You *have been* my *employee*," he drawled, "you became *my love*, and now, you're my prisoner."

He chuckled and snuggled closer to me. I couldn't tell him... not now, not like this. We were so comfortable, so in love.

'Just a few days more,' I thought, 'just a few more days to enjoy this.'

I smiled and snuggled back into him. He used the arm that was wrapped over me to turn me over so that I was facing him. I giggled as he sleepily blinked at me, then pressed a kiss to my lips.

"Your lips are so soft," he murmured sleepily, "I could kiss them all day."

"You're so cute when you're half asleep like this." I giggled.

We continued like that for some time, until one night when Matt began lashing about in his sleep. He woke me with his movements, forcing me to sit up. I shook him awake, shushing him as I did so.

"Hush, hush, now, it's okay," I soothed, "it was just a bad dream... a dream, okay? None of it was real, I promise."

Matt blinked awake; his eyes filled with tears. He was shaking as he embraced me tightly. He muttered something unintelligibly, but I understood what he meant. I had heard of the Intergalactic Wars and the way he had fought in them. I knew that those wars had come with a price far higher than I could ever imagine.

"If I could, I would kiss away all your scars." I told him softly.

I only hoped that my kiss, my love, could heal the scar that would form the moment I confessed my crimes against his organization. It was possible that my guilt over what I planned to do was somehow, subconsciously affecting him and his pain was all my fault. I couldn't let this go on any longer... I had to tell him tomorrow.

The next day after his work ended, Matt stormed into the penthouse. He looked disheveled and stressed, more so than I had ever seen him. His eyes met mine and he stopped in his tracks, remaining silent as he stared at me.

"I've had a rough day and honestly," Matt sighed, "all I want right now is a drink and someone to cuddle with."

Alright, maybe today was not the day to confess my crimes.

"I'll get you something." I rose from my seat and walked to the kitchen.

I brought his drink back to the main living room, where he was now seated. I handed him the drink before sitting by his side. Matt sipped the drink for a few moments, then wrapped his arm around my shoulders.

"What happened?" I asked.

"Just a rough day," he sighed, "apparently there were unauthorized downloads from my holocomp... I'm not sure if I made a mistake or if there was a data breach."

He took a deep breath while I held mine. I wanted to reassure him, but I wasn't sure I could do that without lying to his face. All I could do was cuddle into him as he sipped his drink. I knew there was no other choice now, I had to tell him tomorrow; and this tomorrow could not turn into another tomorrow like it had so many times in the past few weeks.

I knew I was being selfish trying to talk myself out of telling him. We'd had a month of happiness together and that was more than I could have ever hoped for. If I wanted this to continue, especially without any guilt interfering, I needed to tell him.

As soon as he stepped through the door the next day after work, I rushed to him. He looked startled, but not unhappy. Before he could say anything, I started talking.

"I have a confession to make." I said.

"Okay." He looked at me expectantly.

I took a deep breath, trying to figure out how to say it in a way that would hurt him the least. I knew it had to be said, but I didn't want it to harm him more than it had to.

"You know I'm always here for you... right?" he asked, "no matter what."

I looked up, into his eyes. His eyes were full of kindness and sincerity. How could I confess what I had done now?

"Please... talk to me about it," he urged, "whatever it is."

"Do you love me?" I asked tearfully.

"You know I love you." He replied, his brows furrowed.

"And you know I love you," I said, "right?"

"I know," he frowned, "what is going on?"

"I did something bad," I stammered, "and I planned to do something worse."

"Okay." He returned.

"I wasn't chosen completely by chance," I told him, "As soon as I heard that the Intergalactic Endeavour was coming to Ai'Windel, I prepared."

He gave me a questioning look; he was not yet angry or sad, just confused.

"I made myself more attractive in an attempt to seduce my way through the Intergalactic Endeavour," I explained, "I wanted to find a way to the top... to you, so I could take over your organization."

I took a deep breath before continuing, praying for the strength to make my full confession.

"I was the one who broke into your office and downloaded your files," I confessed, "I haven't done anything with them... but I did plan to."

He blinked in shock at me. I waited for an answer which never came. All he did was stand up and leave the room. When night fell, I realized that he was not returning to me with his answer any time soon.

The first night, I was so nervous and upset that I made myself sick. I spent the night mostly in the bathroom, remembering how nice it had been when Matt had helped me when I was sick on the ship. The lonely feeling in my stomach made me feel even worse.

I was alone for a total of 32 days, wondering where he had gone and what would happen to me. Fortunately, food was still delivered for me and the penthouse was so large that I did not get sick of it, nor did I get bored. The only issue I ran into was loneliness, an extreme kind which I had never felt before.

The only reason I lasted such a long time with such little mental distress was the schedule that I had set out for myself. I occupied myself with watching things on the holoprojector, working out in the gym, and creating new recipes from the food in the penthouse. It kept me occupied and most importantly, it kept me from losing my mind.

When Matt walked through the door on the 49th of Peura, I nearly ran into his arms, forgetting what had transpired between us. He didn't look angry anymore, which gave me a little bit of hope. Still, I did not dare to approach him.

"Astra." He said softly.

"Matt?" I returned.

He stepped towards me, slowly and carefully.

"I've decided that while I do not agree with your views or your plan," he said, "I do love you, and I will stay by your side no matter what."

I nodded, unsure of what to say. Mostly, I was confused as to why it had taken him this long to realize this.

"I'm going to listen to what you have to say," he continued, "and I'm going to accept your input. I will make... certain changes that you want to make."

I ran to him and threw my arms around his neck, nearly lifting off the ground as I embraced him. He wrapped his arms around me in return, his warmth enveloping me.

Chapter Seven: A New Beginning

Matt and I attended a meeting with other high-ranking individuals on Sugsa 1, 5020 to plan for the changes we would make. After Matt returned from work, we started our own private meetings.

"What issues do you have with the Intergalactic Endeavour?" Matt asked.

His question, though professional in words, seemed to be emotional in meaning. He was not speaking to me as a colleague; he was speaking to me as one concerned for their partner and their feelings.

"Your question answers itself, or rather, the name does," I replied, "the Intergalactic Endeavour endeavors to accomplish intergalactic power."

"Is that a bad thing?" he frowned.

That question had never been posed to me in my entire life. On Ai'Windel, we prized peace and compassion very highly. In our views, the Intergalactic Endeavour was unempathetic and rough, not caring what harm they caused. Perhaps this was not how the members of the Intergalactic Endeavour saw themselves, though.

"It's not necessarily a bad thing," I answered carefully, "it's the way you're doing it."

"So, what would you have us do?" he questioned.

"I'll need more information to answer that," I said, "I never looked at the files I downloaded... but I know that you have a plan for each of the ten planets in the galaxy."

"Look at the files, then." He responded.

I slunk off to the extra bedroom and rifled through my things until I caught hold of the holodrive. Timidly, I stepped back into the main living room and plugged the holodrive into the holoprojector. Matt moved the remote, selecting the files which would reveal their plans to me.

"I'm curious," he said as he flipped through the files, "where did you hide this?"

"In my boots from Ai'Windel." I replied sheepishly.

He nodded, not removing his eyes from the projection in front of us. I did wonder why he asked such a question, but I decided it was best not to interrogate him.

"At least I know I can trust you not to go through my things," I chuckled, trying to lighten the mood, "otherwise, you would have found it easily."

Finally, the file appeared in the projection before us. I scanned over the document, at the top of which was Ai'Windel. There was a list of objectives for each planet, and I had to read them all at least twice to understand their meaning. Ai'Windel's name and objectives were red and "TERMINATED" was written in bold at the end.

"Terminated?" I questioned.

I was sure that it meant that the plan had been terminated, but I wanted to ensure its meaning. If the word had another meaning, there would definitely be trouble between us once more.

"We terminated our plan after you agreed to come with us... to come with me." Matt explained.

I smiled and wrapped my arm around his, relieved by his answer. He scrolled to the next planet; Doune. I had heard of Doune from Protestor loyalists, who went there to hide from the Intergalactic Endeavour. The planet's name and objectives had been highlighted in green and at the end was written the word "SUCCESS".

The eight other planets followed these. The third was Heloha, a wealthy city planet which had been allied with the Intergalactic Endeavour for some years. The fourth was Intersina, a snowy planet that had been conquered to serve as weapons vault. The fifth planet on the list, Locdu, had a considerably longer list.

OBJECTIVE ONE: RECONAISSANCE

OBJECTIVE TWO: RAID

OBJECTIVE THREE: CONQUER FOR WEAPONS FACTORY

OBJECTIVE FOUR: APPOINT LEADERSHIP

Manno, the next planet, had a similar list of objectives, only the third was "OCCUPY FOR ALLIES". Meiana had the exact same list of objectives as Manno. It was not until I reached Okga that I saw the most horrifying objective: "DESTROY." Beneath this objective was an explanation which was essentially "to send a message to the galaxy."

"You'd destroy a planet," I scoffed, "just to send a message to the rest of the galaxy?"

He gave me an odd look, as if he wasn't sure what I meant.

"That is certainly the first thing I'd like to change." I said.

My eyes shifted to the next planet, Olkana, which had no list of objectives.

"Nothing for Olkana?" I asked.

"It's an uninhabited volcanic planet," Matt explained, "there is little we could hope to do."

"Or you could use it as a Weapons Factory," I retorted, "instead of uprooting millions from their home."

My eyes drifted to the last planet on the list, Seva. There were no objectives, since it had already been conquered as the Intergalactic Endeavour's base planet. I realized, though, that I knew very little of this planet that I now inhabited.

"I want to tour Seva, *really* tour it" I said, "and the rest of the planets. I want to see firsthand what must be done."

"As you wish." He replied.

We set out early the next morning for an in-depth tour of Seva. We walked downstairs hand-in-hand, past Miss Diu's desk. She gave us a malicious look, obviously upset by my apparent success.

"Miss Diu." Matt greeted her.

"Supreme Commander," she returned, "are you sure about giving a tour to *her*?"

My focus was pulled back to Matt, who looked somewhat flustered. If he had told her about my plan, which I now suspected he had, our relationship would forever be tainted. More concerning though, was the possibility that Matt had been with Sara since he left me. Had he only spoken to her as a colleague, I would be slightly less bothered; but if he had been with her in another way, I doubted I could forgive him with ease.

"We'll be back soon." Matt snapped.

Matt pulled me forcefully away from her. I knew that something was going on and that it needed to be addressed, but I decided to focus on the informative tour instead. To do so, I pushed my feelings down until I felt numb, allowing me to pay attention to nothing but the planet.

Seva was beautiful and, according to Matt, very prosperous. It was not nearly as natural as Ai'Windel was, but it was not any less beautiful. Thoughts about what could be done flooded my mind until we returned to the penthouse that evening.

"You do not like Seva?" Matt asked.

"What?" I returned.

"You seemed... disturbed by it." He said.

"Seva is lovely," I replied, "the perfect planet for a base."

There was a long pause.

"What would you change about it, then?" he inquired.

"Nothing." I replied.

Another long pause ensued.

"So, what is wrong?" he questioned.

I considered whether or not I wanted to open the floodgates. Would I be able to control myself or would I lose my composure as soon as I spoke about what was bothering me? I decided against saying anything.

"What planet will we visit next?" I asked.

"Astraella." Matt snapped.

"I want to see Doune," I continued, ignoring him, "I've heard a lot about it."

Matt stepped in front of me and placed his hands on my arms. I looked up at him, trying to defy him with my eyes.

"Tell me what's bothering you." He requested.

"You were with Sara Diu," I said, "after you left."

He was silent as he stared down at me.

"And you told her everything." I hissed.

I pushed his arms off me and stormed off to the extra bedroom. After we looked at the file yesterday, I had snuck the holodrive back into the room, this time hiding it in the pocket of my dress. I stuck the holodrive into my holocomp and downloaded the files. As soon as they were done, I opened my email and crafted a message to my family members.

"If anything happens to me," I whispered as I typed, "take these files to the Protestors."

I sent the message, then stuffed the holodrive back into my dress pocket. I felt somewhat guilty for what I was about to do because, despite my hurt and anger, I still cared about Matt. However, I needed to make a choice sooner rather than later; did I care more about the galaxy or Matt?

“For the galaxy.” I said to myself.

I picked up the knife I had stolen from the kitchen after Matt had left. Its intended purpose was for protection in the event that something happened while he was gone, but now it would serve a different purpose. At least, that was what I thought at first.

It was not until I was at the door that I realized that all the lights, even the motion-triggered lights that bordered the floors, were off. Matt had gone to sleep and had not been out for at least an hour. My chance of threatening him or else assassinating him had past, at least for the night.

Just as I was about to stumble off to bed, the motion-sensor lights turned on again. Thinking I had been given another chance, I hurried towards the door. However, the footsteps were much lighter than Matt's were. In fact, the person moving outside sounded nothing like Matt. Someone was in here and what their plans were, I did not know.

The intruder's footsteps faded, and I cracked the door open to peek outside. Sara Diu was stepping lightly around the penthouse, making her way towards Matt's bedroom. I tiptoed out of my bedroom and towards Sara. She seemed to hear me as I inched closer, since her posture stiffened significantly. Finally, when I was only inches from her, she turned abruptly.

"Astrael..." she started.

I had swooped my arm up to protect myself, unintentionally stabbing Sara in the gut. Her eyes widened, as if she had only just realized what had happened. She moved, either to remove the knife from her abdomen or to attack me. With no way of knowing her intentions, I pushed the knife deeper into her.

After what seemed like forever of staring into her dark, almond shaped eyes, she fell to her knees before me. Blood was pooling at our feet, bathing my toes in red. Her face held a thousand emotions as the life disappeared from them, the most prominent of which were betrayal and despair. Finally, she slumped over, her lifeless corpse a vivid reminder of what I had done.

"Oh, God," I whispered, "I swear I didn't... please forgive me."

My body shook as I thought about what I should do next. The truth was, I couldn't think of a single solution. I needed help, desperately.

"Matt!" I yelled, falling back onto the wall.

It took a moment, but I eventually heard Matt's footsteps coming towards us. He gasped in surprise when he saw Sara's body, then took a minute or two to process it. I didn't know if he was going to condemn my actions; if so, I should certainly run away. Where would I go, though? I could never escape Matt, not while he was Supreme Commander.

"Astra, what did you do?" he breathed.

"I didn't know..." I stammered, "I just... she scared me.... I thought I was defending..."

For some reason, I thought he didn't look nearly surprised enough. Had he expected her to be here? Had he expected me to kill her? Had he expected both?

"What was she doing here?!" I near screamed.

"Hush, someone will hear!" he hissed.

"And what will we do when someone finds out?" I asked.

I crumpled down onto the floor and hugged my knees. I was going to be ill from the stress, I just knew it. To make matters worse, I was now bathed in the blood of my victim. I looked and felt the part of a murderer.

"I'll never get to change the Intergalactic Endeavour now," I whimpered, "all of my work down the drain... my life goal forever incomplete.... just because I killed some stupid homewrecker!"
"While I'm a bit concerned that's your first thought after murdering my secretary," he said, "I disagree that this will ruin things."
"What do you mean?" I asked, tears streaming down my cheeks.
"We can use this for our goals." He grinned, squatting down to me.

I frowned at him, partially wondering what he meant and partially in awe of how he had said "our goals". There was also the fact that he was grinning while kneeling next to his dead secretary and former lover. Actually, everything about this scenario was freaking me out.

"We could say that Diu was our enemy, who came to assassinate us," Matt said, "we will then announce that we will be making changes to the Intergalactic Endeavour as a result."

As I processed what he had said, a smile began to form on my face. They were no longer my goals that he disagreed with, but our goals, which we would work together to implement. Not only that, my enemy and competitor was now gone, her death serving the purpose of fulfilling our goals. Perhaps my mistake, my sin, was a fulfillment of God's plan. Was that even possible, though? After all, it wasn't intentional sin; I thought I was defending myself and had panicked. Alright, maybe this wasn't so bad after all.

"We'll need to call guards soon," I told him, "Or they'll be suspicious."

"And you need to look sadder." He chuckled.

I nodded, plastering a pout on my face. Matt laughed as he stood up, offering me his hand. I allowed him to help me to my feet, still reeling.

"You're going to get sick, aren't you?" he asked, studying my face.

"Probably." I chuckled.

"Go clean up, then sit on the bed and lock the door," he said, "I'll get the guards and take care of everything."

I took his hand in mine and pressed my lips to his hand, before following his orders. I had some suspicions that this had all been a trick, but I could not act on them, as I begun to feel nauseous from the stress. Matt returned with the guards soon enough and I suppressed my gagging long enough to hear him weave a tale of how Miss Diu had tried to assassinate the both of us.

Once I was sure of my safety, I hurried off to the restroom. The sickness did not last as long as I had expected, since Matt had calmed me before I could really let the stress affect me. Still, I did not feel well enough to sleep until Matt returned to inform me that the guards had taken care of Sara's body and sounded the alarm.

"I know you probably don't need more stress right now," he said, stroking my hair, "but we will need to give a speech tomorrow on the event. We really need to use this situation to our advantage as soon as possible."

"I understand." I nodded.

"Are we okay now?" he asked.

"Um..." I trailed off.

"What is it?" he pressed.

"There are some things I need to ask you first," I said, "before I can really... be okay."

Matt raised his eyebrows, urging me to continue.

"Why did you go to Sara Diu after you left me?" I questioned.

"I needed a place to stay," he answered, "it would have been unprofessional for me to stay with a close colleague like one of the Generals. I know... knew Miss Diu well and there were no professional conflicts."

"And what did the two of you do?" I pressed.

"What do you mean?" he frowned.

"Did you sleep with her?" I asked, "or did you just tell her all my secrets?"

"That's why you're upset," he sighed, "you're jealous."

"Answer the question." I demanded.

"I didn't sleep with her," he said, "and the only reason I spoke of you was because I was so upset. Did you expect *me* to keep my feelings to myself all that time?"

He chuckled at his self-deprecating joke, watching for my reaction. I truly couldn't blame him for expressing himself to Sara when he was upset, especially since he had been so honest with me when I'd asked him. I wondered if I should tell him about the email I had sent. I decided against it, since it would probably not be relevant unless something happened to me. If something did happen to me, then Matt would probably deserve it anyways.

"Will you forgive me?" he asked, "can we be together?"

"Now and forever." I smiled, kissing him.

I knew that tomorrow would be the beginning of the new Intergalactic Endeavour... *our* Intergalactic Endeavour.

"I love you." He grinned.

"I love you." I echoed.

The next morning, Matt and I prepared for the speech he was to give. He had offered me a portion in which to speak, but I had refused. I didn't want to compromise the mission, nor did I want to relive what had happened the previous night. I would simply stand at his side in support of him.

"Good morning to the galaxy," Matt began, "I bring you grave news from the base of the Intergalactic Endeavour on the planet of Seva."

He turned to me and held out his arm. I walked towards him, praying that I didn't trip. I thought to myself that perhaps I did deserve to trip and embarrass myself, after what I had done. However, I did not trip, and I ended up at the center of the stage at Matt's side. My lack of tumbling encouraged me in my belief that my sins had been forgiven.

"Last night, the Supreme Companion and I were attacked by Sara Diu." He announced.

There was a gasp from the crowd before us and whispers began to fill the silence. Some of them looked at Matt and some of them looked at me, making me very conscious of my facial expressions.

"Supreme Companion Astraella Wander protected both of us," Matt continued, "and Sara Diu is now dead."

Everyone fell silent again and I could now feel all their eyes on me. I kept my eyes fixed on Matt, hoping I was not about to be persecuted for what I'd done. I deserved it, certainly, but I didn't want it.

"Sara Diu has been officially labelled a traitor to the Intergalactic Endeavour," he said, "and Astraella Wander will from henceforth be known as a Hero of the Intergalactic Endeavour."

Scattered applause sounded from the crowd. It was obvious that they were unsure of me and my actions.

"As such, a few changes will be made to the Intergalactic Endeavour," he declared, "including a new plan for the planets in the galaxy."

He looked over at me and smiled. I nodded back, urging him on despite my fears.

"Violence will no longer be a first option, but a last resort," he finished, "and all the residents of the galaxy will be treated more fairly. The confrontation between the traitor and the Supreme Companion has informed me that this is of paramount importance."

Everyone stared at Matt. Some looked as if they approved while others did not seem pleased. Matt looked to me, and I shuffled closer to him, so that my voice would be projected by the microphone.

"For the galaxy." I said timidly.

Some seemed inspired, while others glared at me.

"For the galaxy!" Brigadier Tenn repeated.

"For the galaxy!" General Porter echoed.

I should have known that these two women would be my first supporters. They had always been so kind to me and seemed to like both me and my ideas. If nothing else, at least I would have their support.

"For the galaxy!" a few more joined in.

Soon, most of the crowd was repeating my mantra enthusiastically. Others still glowered at me, but I knew that our supporters far outweighed our foes, especially if one were to count those across the galaxy who had previously been slighted by the Intergalactic Endeavour.

Matt and I left the stage as the crowd began to calm. We hurried back to the penthouse, where we prepared for the inevitable meetings and ate lunch. I was so excited I could barely stay still as we ate.

"Nervous?" Matt smirked.

"Excited." I corrected him.

He grinned at me and I at him. Had I been sharing this day, this victory, with anyone else, I would have been sorely disappointed. However, sharing it with this brown-eyed, lanky man with a dimpled smile was the best-case scenario for me.

Although it was very unprofessional of us, we walked hand-in-hand towards the meeting room for the higher-ups. The meeting room was one floor below Matt's penthouse and was in a secluded area of the base. Brigadier Tenn, General Porter, and General Uxe, among others, were already seated around the large, oval, table. They all stood upon our entrance, although a few of them did not look pleased about it.

"Good afternoon." Matt greeted them.

Scattered replies sounded around the room. Matt led me to a set of chairs at the end of the table and pulled one of them out for me. I sat down, allowing him to push the chair in behind me. He made his way to the other chair and sat. It seemed that my sitting before him, and thus everyone else, angered some of them even more.

"We'll start right away," he said, "we have a lot to cover today."

As Matt sat down, he pushed a button and a holoprojection appeared before us. Everyone else sat back down, their eyes now fixed on the holoprojection before us.

"As we've already discussed," Matt continued, "Ai'Windel will be left alone."

"Because of your girlfriend." An older man interjected.

I turned my eyes to the aged man, then back to Matt. Matt's eyes were cold and emotionless as he stared at the man. I could have easily defended myself both intellectually and physically, but it was evident from Matt's expression that doing so was unnecessary.

"Anyone who has a problem with the Supreme Companion," he announced, "is free to leave this meeting and the Intergalactic Endeavour immediately."

A few of the older men in the room stood up. Most of the people remained seated, but the fact that a few had stood stung. Did I really have so many enemies in such a short amount of time? I had hardly done anything since I'd arrived.

"Please be advised, however," Matt said, "that you will not be welcomed back if you choose to leave. You will be considered an enemy of the Intergalactic Endeavour."

Some of the men sat, but three of them remained standing, including the man who had spoken earlier. The man left, followed by the others who were still standing. General Uxe stood up abruptly as they exited. He looked at Matt and I, sighed deeply, then sat back down.

"Something to say, General?" Matt challenged.

"No, Supreme Commander." Uxe replied.

I watched him as his gaze fell from Matt to the table before him. It was suspicious that he had even thought of walking out, but I supposed that it was good that he had decided to stay. Regardless, I knew we needed to keep an eye on him. In fact, I probably needed to watch all of the men who had disapproved of me but had been scared into submission by Matt's threats.

"Doune will remain as is," Matthew continued, as if nothing had happened, "but we will be visiting it to ensure good relations. The same will be done for Heloha."

Everyone nodded in agreement, their eyes once more fixed on the holoprojection.

"Intersina will be re-evaluated, to ensure that a livable planet is not being misused," he explained, "and Olkana will be made suitable for a new or additional weapons vault."

"Is that wise, Supreme Commander?" General Porter spoke up, "Olkana is volcanic... unsuitable for life."

Matt looked at me, waiting for me to respond. I hadn't really been prepared to speak out so soon at these meetings, but I knew it was important for me to do so.

"We believe that certain measures can be taken to ensure the safety of individuals working there," I replied, "and it will be more suitable, since we will not be uprooting any natives or anyone who might be able to live there permanently."

I looked back to Matt and nodded for him to continue.

"We will visit Locdu, Manno, Meiana, and Okga and attempt to ally with them," Matt said, "we will want as many planets as possible to be on our side."

"Surely you two don't think that all the planets can be converted." Uxe replied.

"Of course not," I answered, "but the more, the better, right?"

"I suppose." Uxe sighed.

"General Porter, General Uxe," Matt said, "you will be joining us on a trip to Doune tomorrow."

They both nodded in acknowledgement, and General Porter shot me a friendly smile.

"The following week we will visit Heloha," he continued, "and arrangements for trips to the rest of the planets will be made later."

I wondered why he had seemed to skip over the plans to visit Ai'Windel future. Surely, we would be visiting it as well. After all, it was important to keep them on our side; they would not be won over just because I was the Supreme Companion now. Matt continued to speak as I sorted through these thoughts, and he wrapped up the meeting before I could come to a solid conclusion.

"What about Ai'Windel?" I asked as we exited.

"What about it?" Matt returned.

"We will visit it," I said, "won't we?"

"I wasn't planning on it." He shrugged.

"But we'll need them on our side." I frowned.

"That's why we have you." He smiled.

"They will not rally behind us," I said, "just because of me."

He seemed to think for a moment, then looked back at me.

"We will visit it," he told me, "But we should make it a last priority."

His answer, while better than I had expected, made me a bit sad. I missed my home and my family, and I wanted to go back. Matt seemed to pick up on this and he grabbed my hand, giving it a gentle squeeze.

"It's important we don't show partiality to Ai'Windel," he said, "you understand that, don't you?"

"Yes, I suppose." I sighed.

"I'll get you back there as soon as possible." He smiled.

I smiled back, but I didn't feel any better. He was on board with my new ideas, but I wasn't sure that he really cared about what we were doing. If this was going to be a success, that needed to change. Though I obviously wasn't doing the best in terms of getting people behind me, I did know that no one would support us if they could tell we didn't actually care.

The next morning, Matt, General Porter, General Uxe, and I set out for Doune. I was beyond excited to finally visit the planet, especially since it would be the third planet I had ever been on. As we arrived, I saw that my excitement was justified; Doune was unlike anything I had ever seen before.

While Ai'Windel and Seva were green and lush, Doune was dry and brown... a desert of a planet. The sky was a brighter blue than any I'd ever seen, contrasting the sandy ground. White, fluffy clouds floated above us, occasionally blocking one of the four huge moons. High, spiky buildings were set against the backdrop, the only sign of civilization on the planet.

"We'll be meeting with General Kanata in about 15 minutes," Matt whispered to me, "in that building right there."

He pointed to the tallest building, the point of which seemed to reach the sky.

"Then who will we meet with?" I inquired.

He frowned down at me, his eyes full of confusion.

"What do you mean by that?" he asked.

"I mean when are we meeting with the people?" I pressed, "like the leaders of the Protestor gangs?"

"Protestor gangs?" he furrowed his brows, "what do you mean by 'Protestor gangs'?"

"Many Protestors flee here to escape the Intergalactic Endeavour," I explained, "most of them are part of a gang or become part of a gang shortly after arrival."

He looked ahead of him at the buildings, as if he was lost in thought. It seemed that the Intergalactic Endeavour had no idea that the Protestors came here to hide from them, which was exactly what they would have wanted. Unfortunately, I had just revealed their secret to the Supreme Commander, but I hoped that wouldn't be an issue with the changes we were trying to implement.

"We'll discuss that with General Kanata." He finally replied.

We walked into the building and went up to one of the meeting rooms. The meeting with General Kanata was rather boring and seemed to be completely pointless. Kanata gave us a status update, which was mostly finance-based. When Matt asked about the Protestor gangs, Kanata simply brushed off the question and said everything had been peaceful since their last visit.

"I still think we should talk to the people here." I whispered to Matt as we left.

"Why?" he frowned, "General Kanata doesn't seem worried."

"If we want an entire planet on our side," I said, "we can't just make the *leaders* happy."

"But the leaders are all that matter." He returned.

I scoffed and rolled my eyes at his ignorance. He had been in the military and in politics for far too long.

"Fine, I'll do it myself." I dropped his hand and walked away.

It did not take long for me to spot the leader of a Protestor gang. I introduced myself, conveniently leaving out the fact that I was the Supreme Companion of the Intergalactic Endeavour. I only hoped that they did not see any news involving me from the Intergalactic Endeavour.

"Are you from around here?" the gang leader asked.

His question seemed genuine, convincing me that they truly did not know who I was.

"I'm from Ai'Windel, actually," I answered, "I'm just visiting."
"I'm surprised the Intergalactic Endeavour allowed travel here." Another chimed in.
"Special circumstances," I smiled, "so, anything interesting I should know about Doune while I'm here?"
"Stay away from the tall buildings," the leader said, "especially if you're an enemy of the Intergalactic Endeavour. The leadership they've appointed here does not take kindly to those outside the organization."
"Well, my planet is neutral to them," I chuckled, "you are all against the Intergalactic Endeavour?"

I knew the answer to my question, of course, but I couldn't let them know that. In response, they all pulled their vests back to reveal the Protestor emblem.

"Oh, Protestors," I nodded, "I'm curious... why are the Protestors so against the Intergalactic Endeavour?"
"They steal from normal people, like us," the leader answered, "land, food, money, human beings, even."

"Human beings? I wasn't aware..." I began.

"That the Intergalactic Endeavour uses forced labor?" another finished, "most aren't."

Matt had never mentioned that to me, nor had I seen any evidence of it, neither on the Intergalactic Endeavour's base nor from Protestors who had visited Ai'Windel.

"That's... really eye-opening," I said, "um, thank you."

I turned and walked back to Matt, General Porter, and General Uxe, who were fortunately out of sight of the Protestors. We boarded the ship in silence, but I could sense Matt's eyes on me. The ship doors closed behind us, closing us off from the rest of Doune.

"What happened?" Matt whispered.

"Do you enslave people?" I snapped.

His eyes widened and his brows furrowed. It was as if he had no idea what I was talking about. I thought, however, that he must be aware of something so substantial.

"Enslave people?" he scoffed.

"The Protestors said the Intergalactic Endeavour uses forced labor," I said, "as well as stealing land, food, and money from citizens... but that I already knew about."

"We... don't use forced labor," General Porter chimed in, "but... the loyal planets *do* send in volunteers periodically."

"And you reward them for each volunteer?" I questioned.

General Porter nodded and I turned my gaze to Matt. It was evident that he had realized the problem and that it had never occurred to him before.

"Send a message to General Volantes," Matt said, "the Intergalactic Endeavour will henceforth be stopping the Intergalactic Volunteer Program. Broadcast it."

With that, Matt turned and left the rest of us in the cockpit. I looked to General Porter, who seemed to share my thoughts. General Uxe, on the other hand, seemed lost in his own thoughts about the situation. He had been a frightening presence to me ever since he stood up to leave during our meeting. The others who had been against me seemed to have mellowed, but he seemed to be bubbling with thoughts and emotions.

I left them to find Matt, who had shut himself in one of the rooms. I silently entered and sat down next to him, placing a hand on his shoulder. He was not crying or showing any emotion on his face, but I could tell that he was upset.

"What's wrong?" I asked.

"How is it you're better at this than I am?" he scoffed, "I've been in the military more than half of my life, and in politics even longer."

"I've been planning a takeover since I could talk," I laughed, "I've had plenty of time to think about things like this. Besides, I've spent over 20 years being a normal human; you've spent over 20 years dealing with political issues, not people."

"How did I miss something like that?" He sighed, "it's so obvious."

"You're busy with other things," I said, "anyways, it doesn't matter. We're a team now, aren't we?"

I took his hand and offered him the kindest smile I could muster. He smiled back at me and squeezed my hand.

"We're going to change the galaxy." I told him.

Once we were back on base and settled, we made plans for our next trips. The second visit we made was to Heloha. There wasn't much to do there, since everyone there had benefitted from the Intergalactic Endeavour and was therefore completely loyal to them. The only issue we had was that some were upset because of the disbanding of the Intergalactic Volunteer Program. This was not too problematic, though, since they all had plenty of wealth to live off of.

Olkana was next and was evaluated to be the new weapons vault. It was perfect, as we had hoped, and plans were drawn up. Intersina followed, and they were all too happy to go along with our plan to move the weapons vault to Olkana, since they greatly benefitted from the disbanding of the Intergalactic Volunteer Program. They were free to continue producing for the Intergalactic Endeavour, but they were no longer required to do so, which seemed to motivate them even more.

The only neutral planet besides Ai'Windel, the planet Meiana, was our fifth trip. The peaceful planet reminded me of Ai'Windel, but I had to admit it was much prettier than my home planet. It was filled with bioluminescent plants and animals, which filled the entire planet with a beautiful glow.

"I want to stay here a while." I told Matt.

"There is not much to do," Matt replied, "there is no reason for us to stay."

"It reminds me of home," I said, "and it is so beautiful."

"We can spare another day." He acquiesced.

And so, we did. We slept in a beautiful bungalow by the ocean, our last night of rest before our real work began. In the following days, we visited the three remaining planets, the ones which were resistant to the Intergalactic Endeavour.

Locdu, the icy planet known for its dangerous races, was easy to convince after a sizable donation was made. Manno, a beautifully tropical planet, took a bit more time, but after hearing about the changes we were making, they sided with us. Okga was the last planet we visited, and that, coincidentally, was where all the trouble began.

Chapter Eight: The War

People watched us with great interest as we walked through the streets of Okga. People usually watched us, but this was different. Their gazes were intent, malicious. Matt motioned for the guards we had brought along to provide more cover, which they did immediately. As they moved to protect us, people surrounding us started to attack. The guards rushed us back to the ship, sustaining only minor injuries.

"How did this happen?" Matt huffed, "no one but those a part of the Intergalactic Endeavour knew we were coming."

Brigadier Tenn, who was standing in for General Uxe today, was the first to realize, I could tell from her eyes. She seemed almost disappointed in herself, though, as if she should have realized as soon as General Uxe claimed he had suddenly fallen ill and asked her to fill in.

"We have a spy." General Porter said, as if she could read Tenn's mind.

"I think I know exactly who it is." Brigadier Tenn nodded.

"I'm not surprised." I said.

"And I'm going to kill him." Matt added through clenched teeth.

These past two weeks, everything had been suspiciously successful. Those who had left the Intergalactic Endeavour on the first day had been quiet and we had been met with no resistance. It was only logical that they had been hiding out somewhere, waiting for the perfect opportunity to attack.

General Uxe, who had almost left but thought better of it, was obviously the architect of all of this. He had sent intel to the disgruntled former members, informing them that our last visit would be to Okga, and that was where they should hide. Personally, I would not have waited until the Intergalactic Endeavour had so many other planets backing them, but they certainly did have an advantage in terms of information.

"Call the base and have General Uxe held for interrogation," Matt said to the guards, "immediately."

The guards left and I turned to General Porter.

"We should contact the planets we've allied with," I told her, "Before anyone else can get to them... besides, who knows how quickly we are going to need their help."

"Right away, ma'am," Porter nodded, "should I contact Ai'Windel as well?"

"We'll address them in the press conference," I responded, "just focus on the other planets first."

General Porter bowed of the room to do as I had told her.

"Tenn," I said, "we're going to need a press conference and statement prepared. We'll have to start as soon as we get back."

Brigadier Tenn nodded and followed General Porter. Meanwhile, I turned to Matt, who looked both angry and shocked.

"It'll all work out... after all, we are a perfect team," I smiled, trying to take his mind off the situation, "you remembered to take care of General Uxe, while I remembered to take care of the people. General Porter and Brigadier Tenn are loyal and intelligent and supportive, our perfect additions."

"Will what we're doing be enough, though?" He asked.

"We just have to have faith." I said.

Faith had become more important to me than ever after leaving Ai'Windel. My prosperity had blinded me from its value before, but now I realized its momentousness. I had come to the Intergalactic Endeavour with nothing but my faith, which never left me.

We were back to Seva not long after and we were rushed by heavily armed guards directly to the base. There were no threats on Seva that we knew of, but since there was at least one traitor here, we needed the extra protection.

"I'm going to get you settled in the penthouse," Matt said, "and then I'll go deal with the traitor."

It seemed as though Matt could not bear to say his name. He still seemed livid, though the rest of us had calmed down from our excitement on Okga.

"I'll go with you." I offered.

"No, I want you safe." He countered.

"And I want *you* safe." I replied.

"I'll be fine," he stopped at the elevator, "as long as I know you're safe."

He cupped his hand behind my head and pressed a kiss to my forehead. He looked into my eyes, smiled, then turned his gaze to the guards surrounding us.

"Take her up and guard the door," he ordered, "don't let anyone in except for me."

Matt turned on his heel and walked away from us, his steps heavy and deliberate. I reluctantly watched him go, then went with the guards up to the penthouse. I locked myself inside, not completely trusting the guards who stood outside the main door to protect me. With anxiety plaguing my thoughts, I waited impatiently for Matt to return.

I fell asleep before Matt returned and woke to the sound of his heavy boots upon the floor. He walked towards me, his eyes red and puffy from either tears or exhaustion; I couldn't tell which. He gripped a cup tightly in his hand, his knuckles white.

"What happened?" I asked.

"He's been imprisoned for his crimes," Matt answered, "he is awaiting trial."

"When will it be?" I inquired.

"Two days." He replied.

I hugged my knees to my chest, deep in thought about the upcoming trial.

"Have you eaten?" I asked.

"A little." He shrugged.

"Why don't you go shower?" I suggested, "I'll get you something to eat."

He put his cup down on my bedside table and shuffled off to the shower. I made my way to the kitchen, where I made him a small meal that I thought would keep his strength up. Despite this distraction though, I couldn't stop my thoughts from drifting to General Uxe.

By the time I got back, Matt was asleep on the bed, only half-dressed. I went back to the kitchen to put his food on the warmer, then returned to the bedroom. I looked over him, pondering all that we had been through together.

I soon fell into my solace habit, calculating the most arbitrary of things. We had known each other seven months now; that was 343 days out of the 490 days in a year, or approximately 70% of the year. The most surprising thing, though, was that we'd been together so long now, but we'd remained the same in our relationship. We slept next to each other every night and had meals together, but all we even talked about anymore was the Intergalactic Endeavour. I missed how our relationship had been at first; flirty, playful, exciting. I almost wished I had never told him my original intentions and plan.

He looked so attractive laying there, his bare torso moving with every breath. I wondered how upset he'd be if I were to wake him. Part of me wanted to let him rest, but the other part of me just wanted him for myself. Unable to decide whether or not to wake him up, I sat by his side and played with the dark strands of his hair.

"You okay?" he murmured, blinking awake.

I didn't respond, just slid closer to him. He turned over and I moved over him to press a kiss to his lips. He looked surprised but not upset, so I kissed him again for a bit longer this time. His expression remained the same, so I decided it would be best if I left him to sleep.

Matt did not mention what I had done until the next day. He had been watching me closely since I had kissed him, but our conversations were insufferably normal. The only sign anything was happening, although it was subtle, was the way he had been smirking at me throughout the day. His taunting smirk reminded me of when we had first gotten together.

"What?!" I finally shouted.

"I know you want to do something." He said.

"I have no idea what you mean." I scoffed.

"Really?" he smirked, "so you climbed on top of me and kissed me yesterday for what? To check my pulse?"

I stammered, looking for an answer. I didn't want him to get the best of me, but I simply couldn't think of anything to say.

"That's what I thought." He chuckled.

Our holopads beeped in perfect sync and we grabbed them in unison.

"Turn on the news?" I read in a confused tone.

Matt was already across the room, fiddling with the holoprojection machine. The news program appeared before us, featuring a smartly dressed woman speaking impassively.

"An anonymous individual from Ai'Windel has released classified Intergalactic Endeavour documents," the woman said, "this comes as a great shock to the galaxy, as it was generally accepted that Ai'Windel was allied with the Intergalactic Endeavour after one of its citizens was chosen as the Supreme Companion."

I was a bit shocked that it was widely known that I was the Supreme Companion. Despite my knowledge that the fact had been revealed on the news across the galaxy, I still held the belief that only those I met in person knew I held the position. The more important piece of information though, was that Intergalactic Endeavour classified documents had been released from Ai'Windel. I, of course, knew exactly how they'd been released, I just didn't know why.

"Astraella?" Matt turned to me.

I could tell from his expression what he was about to say. I had been worried that our relationship was falling apart before, but now I was terrified that our relationship would be ruined. This was all, without a doubt, my fault.

"Did you... did you have anything to do with this?" he asked.

He sounded as if he was on the verge of tears, and I really didn't want to answer.

"Let's just sit down for a minute," I said, "process all of this."

He looked wary, but he eventually sat down with me. I could tell that he suspected what I was about to say, but he didn't want to believe it.

"When I found out you had been with Diu after you left me," I told him, "I was livid... so I sent an email to my family with the files I downloaded from your office. I told them to release them to the Protestors if anything happened to me... I'm guessing they think I'm in danger."

"This didn't come from the Protestors, though." He said.

"They probably just joined forces with the Protestors," I shrugged, "or they got so worried that they just did it themselves."

"This could ruin everything," he hissed, "if they find out what we planned to do before..."

"It's no different from what you were *doing* before!" I retorted.

He huffed and stood up, turning his back to me.

“We’ll make a public statement,” I said, “I’ll tell my family not to do anything else and urge my planet to ally with us. Then, we can tell everyone how and why we’ve changed our plans for the galaxy.”

He was silent for a moment, his shoulders rising and falling as he breathed slowly. His rising anger became evident as he clenched his fists, which only made me angrier.

“If you didn’t want stuff like this to get out,” I snapped, “you shouldn’t have made stuff like this in the first place. Now, are you going to let me help you or not?”
“I’ll arrange the press release.” He said.

With that, he left. He returned an hour later to gather me, and we headed off to the press conference. The audience was full, but the stage was empty, waiting only for me and Matt. I took to the microphone first, knowing that what I said would set the tone for the rest of conference.

"Good morning, everyone," I spoke as clearly as I could, "I wanted to address the recent classified document release from my home planet of Ai'Windel."

Everyone was listening carefully to me, their eyes boring into mine.

"The documents have been made irrelevant, since we have drastically changed both the Intergalactic Endeavour and the galaxy," I continued, "I urge my family and the rest of my people on Ai'Windel not to make war with the Intergalactic Endeavour but to instead ally with them."

People in the room were now frantically scribbling things down and photographing me.

"As you can all see, I am alive and well," I said, "flourishing in my new position in the Intergalactic Endeavour."

I turned to Matt and nodded my head. He approached the microphone, and I stepped to the side to allow him to speak. He gave a more political speech, vowing to send anything required to Ai'Windel to create peace. We had not discussed our speeches beforehand, but they worked perfectly together.

Afterwards, we left together and returned to the penthouse to await the public's reaction. It only took a few hours for them to get ahold of the footage, photographs, and statements from the press conference. It took just as long for them to form an opinion of what we'd said.... and what I'd said.

"Astraella Wander, formerly of Ai'Windel," one news announcer said, "has decided to cut ties with the Protestors and her planet, instead siding with the Intergalactic Endeavour."

"I don't think this is good." I murmured.

Matt wrapped his arm around my shoulders in a comforting gesture as reporters were shown at Ai'Windel.

"What do you think of Astraella Wander?" the reporter asked a citizen.

"I think she's a traitor." The citizen replied.

"Commander's whore!" someone in the background yelled.

Soon, the derogatory phrase was being repeated by everyone surrounding the reporter.

"Great. This is great," I whispered, my voice trembling, "and my parents... what are my parents even thinking of me?"

Matt switched the holoprojector off and turned to me.

"I'm sure General Uxe sent people there," he said, "to ruin the public's opinions of you... of us."

"General Uxe..." I sighed, "I can't go to his trial now."

"Why not?" Matt frowned.

"People are going to side with him," I said, "the judge, the jury, the public... and they'll end up siding with his ideals... they'll be completely against us."

"If you don't go," he retorted, "people will think they've beaten you, they'll think you're weak... and they'll be right."

I frowned up at him, wondering why he was choosing to essentially insult me when I was already feeling so badly.

"What?" I scoffed.

"Avoiding him and the trial will be weak of you," he said, "you need to go if you still want to achieve your goals. You need to send a message."

"Send a message." I repeated.

His words had struck a chord with me. He was right, I needed to send a powerful message.

"I want a dress made for me," I said, "something regal... something similar to your clothing. And I want to walk in front of you."

"That's not really... typical of a Supreme Companion." He replied.

"Exactly... we need to be viewed as equals," I told him, "I can't be viewed as your little captive. That's the only way I can stop seeming like... what they're calling me."

"All right." He sighed.

On Alze 15, the day of General Uxe's trial, I strutted through the doors of the courtroom. Those in the room gasped and their eyes widened as they watched me walk in, before the Supreme Commander and wearing the attire of a queen. I wore a white dress with a cape, the sleeves of which were spiked like they were on Matt's uniform, and I walked in just steps ahead of him, basically asserting my dominance over him. It seemed as if my plan was going perfectly based on the reactions I was getting.

I did not sit down in my place until Matt had joined me, since I did not want to push my luck too far. Once everyone had recovered from my entrance, the trial started. It was rather boring, and I zoned out for the majority of it. Instead, I reveled in the victory I'd had in solidifying my place in the Intergalactic Endeavour.

"The jury will now exit the room to deliberate," the judge announced, "we will reconvene as soon as they come to their decision."

Matt and I exited after the jury and judge did. We were met with curious glances, but not as much interest as before.

"Do you think I ruined everything?" I whispered.

"I doubt anyone cared after the trial began." He shrugged, taking a swig of water.

"So... you think they'll rule in our favor?" I asked.

He took my hand and led me to a bench in a secluded corner. We sat down on the bench, and I gave him an inquisitive look.

"I think... I think we should pray about it," he said, "instead of sitting here worrying about it."

I felt a sudden warmness in my heart. The official religion of the Intergalactic Endeavour was Christianity, and many people followed the religion, but he had never explicitly referenced it. was such a gesture of vulnerability and tenderness that it illuminated my entire soul. He was so incredibly anxious, and he could not handle it on his own.

"Okay." I nodded.

He took my hands in his and softly spoke a prayer, asking God to do what was right, to side with the ones who deserved it. We both thought it was us, the Intergalactic Endeavour, of course, but that didn't mean it was true. It was comforting to know that God would choose the one who truly should succeed.

The trial resumed as soon as we concluded our prayer, almost as if it was a sign from God. The deliberation had been suspiciously short, but certainly not the shortest in the galaxy's history. Still, it was a little concerning. We re-entered the courtroom, which was buzzing with anticipation.

"The jury has reached a decision in the case of Uxe versus the Intergalactic Endeavour," the judge said, "the jury finds Joseph Roq Uxe, former General of the Intergalactic Endeavour, guilty of treason and accessory to murder in the first degree."

Guards moved to take General Uxe, who was shouting something to those surrounding us, something about bringing down the new Intergalactic Endeavour. Meanwhile, everyone else was chatting excitedly about the trial and its outcome.

"The sentence is death by beheading." The judge continued.

The courtroom went completely silent. My stomach turned. My heart clenched.

"Death by beheading?" I whispered to Matt.

He grabbed my hand and squeezed it.

"He was aware of the punishment for traitors." He breathed.

I could tell that Matt was just as shocked as I was, even though he was trying his best to hide it. The courtroom cleared before he seemed to be capable of moving.

"I guess I won't be the most hated one in the galaxy now." I chuckled lightly.

"That depends." He shrugged.

"On?" I asked.

"Whether or not they approve of the jury's decision." He said.

The next day was the day that Uxe was to be executed. It was the subject of intergalactic news and would be broadcasted to everyone in the galaxy. We knew that almost everyone would be watching, so it was important that we portrayed ourselves in a proper manner.

One way in which we were sending a silent message to the galaxy was through our clothing. Matt was wearing a black military uniform with red and white sashes. I wore a bolder outfit; a red dress with sparkling adornments on the bodice and sleeves, a matching cape, and a belt with a gold buckle. This was no time to wear muted colors and simplistic outfits; this was the time to show strength and bravery.

"Ready?" Matt asked me.

"Ready." I echoed.

We stepped outside to the courtyard where Uxe was to be executed. A larger crowd than I had ever seen had gathered to watch and there were cameras all around. This would be the most highly publicized event in the Intergalactic Endeavour event in history and I was going to be present for it.

"We have gathered her today to witness the execution of Joseph Roq Uxe," a preacher announced, "we pray that God will forgive this man of his sins and help him to accept Christ in his heart. We pray that God will deal with graciously and mercifully with us."

I clasped my hands together tightly in front of me, silently repeating the prayer. Matt stepped closer to me, so that I could feel the warmth radiating from his body.

"For his crimes against the Intergalactic Endeavour and its leaders," the judge said, "Joseph Roq Uxe has been sentenced to death by beheading."

Uxe was placed on the block and injected with a fluid which would calm him into sleeping, making the execution a bit more humane. We all watched as he slowly slumped over and his eyes closed. He fought it at first, but he could not fight it forever.

The preacher was handed the Executioner's Sword, which he blessed before handing it to the judge. The judge pursed her lips and walked towards Uxe, slowly and deliberately. She raised the sword, then swung it down towards Uxe's head. I flinched but tried my best to hide it.

Matt grabbed my arm and pulled me back the way we came. I kept a straight face as I walked, aware that all eyes were on me. Guards began to surround us as we walked, although no one seemed to be interested in attacking us at the moment. It was not until we were inside, away from curious eyes, that I allowed myself to cry.

"It's alright, it's alright," Matt said, "let's get back upstairs in case anything happens."

I nodded and allowed him to lead me back upstairs to the penthouse. We were locked inside, safe from anything that might happen now. We would be staying there for the next three days, after which we should be safe. Usually, the emotions and riots that came with events like this subsided after three days.

We started watching the news as soon as we were safely inside the penthouse and did not stop for the entire time we were there. Our windows and doors had been covered with bulletproof screens, so the news was our only view into the outside world. Unfortunately, it was not a beautiful view.

"J-R-U? What does 'jru' mean?" I asked.

"Don't you remember?" Matt replied, "his initials."

"They're supporting him?" I scoffed.

"Some of them," he said, "the official reports show 70% in our favor."

"But 30% in theirs." I added.

"The numbers are in our favor." He shrugged.

"But we'll need everyone in our favor," I said, "if we're really going to change things."

He only turned his attention back to the holoprojection in front of us.

"We'll not get more than 90% of them on our side," he said, "no leader is liked by *everyone.*"

"We'll shoot for the moon and land amongst the stars." I smiled.

If this was only 30% of the galaxy, then we would certainly need more people on our side.

Chapter Nine: For the Galaxy

On Alze 20th, 5020, we left the penthouse. Protests had been going on for the past three days, but the guards thought it was safe for us to leave now. After all, we had to speak about what had been happening at some point.

Matt was the one who gave the speech, since he was technically the highest-ranking member in the Intergalactic Endeavour, despite my performance at the trial. I simply stood in the background during his speech, watching the reactions of the audience. Almost everyone seemed calm and attentive, except for a few men who were glaring up at us, shifting their weight suspiciously.

I glanced over at the guards, who seemed to be on the same page as me. They subtly stepped into place around us, preparing for the worst. I wasn't too frightened, since there were not many of them and they certainly could not overpower our armed guards, but I was not pleased that such men were still on Seva. By the end of the speech, none of them had made a move, which comforted me somewhat. Then, as Matt stepped back towards me, a man raised his fist.

"For the galaxy!" he shouted.

I looked at the man, who raised his other hand, holding a blastgun, towards Matt. I couldn't think of much in that moment, but I knew that I just couldn't watch him die in front of me, so I jumped in front of him. The next thing I knew, I was thrown into Matt's body. I was unsure of what happened at first, as I hadn't felt anything touch me, but then I felt a burning pain in my shoulder.

I looked up at Matt first and I could see the shock in his face. He placed his hand behind my shoulder, and I turned my head to see blood running down my arm. I frowned at it in confusion, still not fully understanding what had happened. It was not I who had been shot, was it?

"Astra, stay awake, okay?" he stammered.

The guards around us tightened their formation as the crowd clamored.

"Awake?" I mumbled.

I noticed that I was on the ground now, but how I had gotten there I had no idea.

"We need to get her out of here." Matt shouted up at them.

"We can't," one of the guards said, "not until the area is secure."

"Well, then call someone!" he yelled.

I felt very strange suddenly and I closed my eyes, waiting for the sensation to pass.

"Just hold on, okay?" Matt said.

I tried to grab onto his arm, but I couldn't move properly. I tried to say something to him, but I couldn't. I couldn't do anything properly, it seemed. All of a sudden, my body felt weird, like it was floating.

When I opened my eyes, a bright light blinded me. I blinked a few times, trying to figure out what had happened. Had I been shot? Did I bleed out and die right there on the stage? I tried to talk, to cry out for help, but all I could do was cough.

"Are you alright, ma'am?" a woman's voice sounded beside me.

I squinted and looked around until I found the source of the voice; a nurse dressed completely in white.

“What?” I asked.

“You’re moving around a lot,” she said, “is there something you need, ma’am?”

“Uh, where am I?” I stammered.

“Intergalactic Endeavour Base Hospital, ma’am.” she replied.

I was silent for a moment, putting the pieces together slowly.

“Do you want me to summon the Supreme Commander, ma’am?” she inquired.

“Oh, um, yes.” I stammered.

She nodded in acknowledgement and turned around. I tried to sit up and watch her leave but a sharp pain in my back prevented me from doing so. I moved again, trying to figure out where exactly the pain was coming from.

Before I could pinpoint it, the door opened again. Matt, still in his outfit from the speech but looking disheveled, and the nurse, stepped into the bleached room. His face seemed to relax as he saw me, but I could tell that he had been upset from the way his eyes were swollen.

"You *are* still alive." Matt exhaled.

"Don't sound so disappointed," I chuckled, "I might start to think you don't like me."

He didn't laugh at my joke; he only stepped closer to me and took my hand. The nurse bowed her head and crept out of the room.

"Don't you have a galaxy to run?" I asked, trying to suppress a cough.

"My favorite human is in the hospital," he answered, "the galaxy can wait."

"I'm not sure it works like that." I laughed.

"Well, since I run the galaxy," he said, "I say it does."

I shifted uncomfortably, trying to sit up. The pain seemed to be coming from the back of my shoulder, and I wasn't completely sure how I was going to seem normal with such an injury. Still one thought pervaded my mind; he couldn't be doing this, not right now, when we were at such a critical point. Really, neither of us could be doing this; we could not be together if we wanted the Intergalactic Endeavour to survive.

"You should go," I choked out, "we can't be together like this. It's too dangerous."

"What do you mean?" he asked.

"Obviously, this isn't working for you, for me, for either of us," I said, "you need to just... continue with this work and leave me behind. We need to break up whatever this is."

"Do you think I stay because I enjoy this infatuation of mine?" he scoffed, "this horrifying need to know you are okay at all times? This intense love I feel for you?"

"Well, you need to figure out a way to stop it," I returned, "stop caring about me if it's such a problem for you... it's not doing any good for either of us."

"Astraella, I can't just stop caring for you!" he shouted, "and you know, the fact that you can even ask that of me kills me. It shows me just how ignorant you are of the power you have over me."

It was my turn to frown at him. Our relationship had hit a plateau, and any advances had been initiated by me. How could he say he felt so strongly about me when it was obvious that he didn't? Besides, our love was bringing down the galaxy that we both so obviously and so painfully cared for. How could he be so selfish as to even *want* to stay by my side?

Matt's frown faded into an amused expression as he considered my features. Knowing that something in my expression must have betrayed my thoughts, I straightened my features as best I could. Still, his eyes glimmered with mischievousness.

"Don't try to act so blasé," he smirked, "I know how you feel about me."

I couldn't tell him the truth and risk him staying here with me. It was paramount that he returned to his place to take care of the Intergalactic Endeavour.

"I feel nothing for you," I said, "absolutely nothing."

"Is that so?" he moved closer to me.

I knew he could see my heart rate on the screen next to me, so I tried my best to slow my heartbeat.

"Nothing," I breathed, "I only care for the galaxy."

He placed one hand on either side of me on the hospital bed. I swallowed, focused more on keeping my face from reddening than slowing my heart rate. It beeped, alerting us both that my heart rate had reached an unnatural rate.

"Relax, princess, I'm not going to jump on you," he smirked, "not until you're better anyway."

I swallowed as he moved away from me.

"Now that I have your attention," he said, "I should inform you that I've officially named you Supreme Commandress of the Intergalactic Endeavour."

He turned and left just as the nurse entered the room. I knew my mouth was hanging open, but I couldn't seem to change my shocked expression.

"Are you alright, ma'am?" the nurse inquired.

"I'm... I'm the Supreme Commandress of the Intergalactic Endeavour?" I gasped.

"Yes, ma'am." The nurse nodded.

I smiled to myself, a myriad of thoughts running through my head.

"Can you get me my tablet?" I asked.

"Yes, ma'am." She replied.

The nurse reappeared with my tablet promptly, as if she was fearful that I would unhappy if she did otherwise. I really wouldn't have been, but I was certainly eager to start working on my new plan. Matt and I would be equals now, which meant that I could do more...that *we* could do more.

Despite the soreness in my shoulder, I worked tirelessly on my new plan. There was so much to be done, so many laws to be created. My new title, our new level of partnership, would be the first sentence in a new chapter of history.

The plan was finished by the end of the first week and was perfected by the end of the second week. As far as I could tell, I had covered everything that the new Intergalactic Endeavour needed. The next day, I called for Matt so I could present my plan to him.

"You asked to see me?" he said.

"I know you're busy," I began, "what with you re-starting everything."

"What do you need?" he asked, sitting down beside me.

"I've drawn up a new plan for the Intergalactic Endeavour," I told him, "I want you to get started on it for me."

I handed the tablet to Matt and waited for him to look over it. He nodded as he read through, then looked back up at me.

"This is insane," he chuckled, "how long have you been working on this?"

"The two weeks I've been here." I replied.

"You did this in two weeks?!" he exclaimed.

"I had a lot of time on my hands," I laughed, "there's not much to do here."

"Astra, this is... absolutely prodigious." He said.

"Prodigious? I wouldn't go that far." I chuckled.

He looked over it again.

"Will you start implementing it?" I asked, "for me?"

"I will." He leaned in and kissed my cheek.

"Thank you." I smiled.

I rested soundly that night, knowing that I could trust Matt to execute my plan properly. Unfortunately, it meant that Matt was unable to visit me again. It was lonely without him, but it gave me more time to focus on recovering.

"Supreme Commandress," a nurse said, "you have visitors."

"Visitors?" I frowned.

Matt shouldn't have time to visit me, not yet. Even if he did, who would he be bringing with him?

"Yes, ma'am," the nurse replied, "General Porter and Brigadier Tenn, ma'am."

"Show them in." I nodded.

The nurse bowed out of the room and soon returned with Porter and Tenn. I tried to sit up and make myself look as presentable as possible.

"General Porter, Brigadier Tenn," I addressed them, "how nice of you to visit me."

"I would gladly accept the compliment," General Porter replied, "if it were deserved."

"What do you mean?" I chuckled.

"We're here for business." Porter said.

"Business?" I frowned, "what do you mean?"

They both stepped tentatively closer to me and sat down. Porter looked over at Tenn.

"We wanted to let you know, now that you're officially Supreme Commandress," Tenn whispered, "that should you ever choose to rule alone, we would support and follow you wholeheartedly."

I blinked in surprise as they both suspiciously studied our surroundings.

"You mean... if Matt died?" I stammered.

"Or if... he was to be overthrown." Porter added.

Taking power after overthrowing or killing Matticas Damiran would be difficult. Though I had a prominent General and Brigadier bolstering me, I knew gaining support from others would be difficult. Though there were those who did not like the Supreme Commander and the Intergalactic Endeavour, no amount of calumny could get rid of the love that the general public had for Matticas Damiran.

I was ambivalent about their statements and their support. I felt an amalgam of feelings, which seemed to cloud my thinking. Still, two thoughts prevailed in my mind. The first was that Porter and Tenn had told me this to test me, because they thought I was an ingenuous young woman whose loyalties were volatile. The second was that they truly were not devoted to their Supreme Commander and would betray either or both of us in the future. Regardless, there was only one answer I could give.

"I'd like to rule with him," I answered, "not in spite of him."

It seemed to be the most innocuous answer. I was not speaking against Matt, nor was I necessarily speaking in support of him. I expressed my desire to rule with him, but otherwise remained neutral.

"I understand," General Porter nodded, "then we will continue to serve under both of you."

They both exited the room, leaving me alone with my thoughts. Perhaps I should have accepted their offer. After all, I was the one who was making all of these positive changes to the Intergalactic Endeavour. Though Matt had a myriad of supporters, the galaxy needed someone different, someone more sedulous than him.

Still, I loved Matt, and I had no desire to supplant him. He was good-hearted and kind, just somewhat misled. I knew that together we could create the best galaxy ever. That was the key, though: we had to do it together.

Chapter Ten: Home

On the first day of the new month, I celebrated my 30-day anniversary in the hospital. I'd become accustomed to my new schedule by now, and I hardly minded being here. Even better, my shoulder had nearly healed completely.

"Are you ready to go?" Matt asked.

"Go?" I repeated, "go where?"

"Home, Astra." He chuckled.

I had expected him to say that I had to go to yet another test. During the past few days, I'd been subjected to all kinds of tests to make sure I was healing properly and not getting infections.

"I'm... I'm good to go?" I asked.

"Actually, you were good to go days ago," Matt said, "I just wanted to make sure nothing happened."

"So, you made me stay here longer than I had to?" I frowned.

He sat down across from me, slowly and solemnly. I had expected one of his usual quips, but he was so suddenly serious.

"I can't lose you, ever," he choked out, "to anything."

I looked at him, waiting for him to continue.

"I thought I'd lost you... before." He said.

"When I was shot?" I frowned.

"They got you in a vulnerable spot," he nodded, "we weren't sure you were going to survive."

I hadn't even considered the possibility of me dying. What would have happened to my family if I had died?

"I want to go home," I said, "to *my* home. To Ai'Windel."

Matt blinked in surprise, then chuckled.

"I hope you mean for a visit," he said, "because I've already arranged that."

"Really?!" I exclaimed, "when do we leave?"

"Ocha 15th." He answered.

"Oh, that's a while away." I sighed.

"Only two weeks, Astra." He laughed.

"Why so long?" I whined.

"I want to be absolutely sure that you don't get any infections." He said.

"It's been 30 days, Matt," I retorted, "I think I'm good."

"You need to make sure you can handle your normal routine first." He argued.

I huffed at him and folded my arms over my chest. I had been exercising with the nurses and doing my normal work; why would he think I couldn't handle my normal routine?

"Come on, let's go home." He offered me his hand.

I rolled my eyes at him, but eventually deigned to take his hand. He treated me like porcelain as he escorted me back to our penthouse, which aggravated me to no end. He had left me under constant medical care for 30 days; there was very little that could happen to me now. I knew he had been scared of losing me, but this really seemed superfluous.

Two weeks later, I was just as well as I had been the day I had left the hospital. Matt had been helping me excessively, making me feel incredibly restive. Still, I was excited to get to finally go home and see my family.

It had been 358 days since I had seen my family and my planet. Communications had been monitored closely since I'd joined the Intergalactic Endeavour, so I hadn't received much from them. I had a few pictures to remind me of their appearance, but not much else.

In one of the faster spaceships, it took us five days to get to Ai'Windel. We arrived on the 20th of Ocha, getting me even closer to the one-year mark of being away from my family. I wondered if this had been done on purpose, to separate my emotions from them and draw me towards the Intergalactic Endeavour.

Ai'Windel was just as beautiful as I remembered it. Shining waterfalls dropped from the mossy floating mountains and glimmering water ran between grassy terrain. The air tasted cool and sweet, like home. The only difference was the rows of people waiting for us. They looked neither irate nor jubilant, merely phlegmatic. I could see my family standing at the end, but Matt's tight grip around my arm prevented me from running to them. He only released me once we had reached them, allowing me to embrace each member of my family.

"Come on." My mother whispered, turning.

We followed them back to my house, which seemed as if it had grown. I realized once we entered it that it *had* expanded since I'd left. They must have used the funding they received to extend the house.

"We missed you." My mother said as soon as the door closed.

She embraced me tightly, kissing the top of my head. Everyone hugged me again, tighter than they had before. I gave them an inquisitive look.

"We can't risk you being out in the open like that," my mother told me, "Not anymore."

"People are still after me?" I looked to Matt.

Matt nodded and looked to the ground, in either fear or shame.

"Well, what am I supposed to do?" I asked.

"Keep going." My father answered.

"Keep fighting." Marsa added.

"Change the galaxy," my mother smiled, "for the better."

I smiled at my family, glad that they did not resent me for my time away and my focus on political pursuits.

"Shall we sit and discuss the way forward?" Matt asked, his eyes locked on me.

I nodded and my family showed us to the newly renovated living room.

"We've made a few of the changes already," I told them, "Given each planet a new purpose, a new responsibility within the galaxy and we've taken steps to prevent slavery within individual planets."

"And you'll be arranging Fair Trade?" Marsa asked.

"Yes, we'll make it a requirement for all goods." I nodded.

"What about the humans?" Olver piped up.

"We'll be rewarding individual volunteers," I said, "not the planets."

"That will probably work better than the alternative." My mother nodded.

"What else are you doing?" my father asked.

"Abolishing the death penalty in favor of less severe punishment," I said, "free education, fact-checking for media."

"And weapons control." Matt added.

I turned to him with a confused look.

"I didn't put that in my plan." I whispered.

"I added it." He replied.

I respected his decision to add something to my government plan, but I was peeved that he hadn't discussed it with me first.

"What are we to do until everything's settled?" my mother inquired.

"I've discussed it with the security team," Matt said, "they agree you should at least stay on planet until things have calmed down. We also think you should lay low for a bit and if you're willing... we have guards ready to protect you."

"Yes," My father interjected, "we'll accept them."

"Well, will it take away from the security for you two?" my mother asked.

"Not at all." Matt shook his head.

"Then, we will accept them." My mother agreed.

Once everything was settled and signed, we retired to the dining room. I noticed as we ambulated through my home that so much had changed. Things had been rearranged to account for the added space, making me feel like a foreigner. Still, there were things that were familiar, like the orbicular white chairs, the golden shelves adorned with spiky stars, the blue globe in the living room, and the blue backsplash in the kitchen that was bedecked with silver atom symbols and stars.

We dined together that night, jovially chatting as if we were not in the midst of war. It was innocuous, I knew, but I couldn't help but feel a twinge of guilt. Even so, I felt as if a weight had been lifted off my shoulders, as if life was back to normal for all of us.

We'd planned to stay until the end of the month, but we were called back on official business. General Porter had contacted us saying that she had urgent news for us, but she would not give us any further details. We knew it must be serious if it was classified and restricted, so we packed up and prepared to return to the Intergalactic Endeavour base.

"You will be back soon, won't you?" Sofi asked.

"As soon as the war is over," I told her, "And everything is settled."

I hugged my family and bid them goodbye, then left with Matt to board the ship home. We arrived back at the base five days later, and were rushed by General Porter and Brigadier Tenn.

"We need to go to the SCIF." General Porter whispered.

We did not say any more, just followed them to the secure room where we could discuss whatever sensitive information they had for us. The four of us hastened towards the SCIF at the center of the base and were locked inside.

"Our soldiers have won great victories for us," General Porter blurted out, "all of our foes have been beaten or captured. The Protestors wish to surrender and swear fealty to the Intergalactic Endeavour."

"We should accept... right?" I looked to Matt.

"What conditions did they give?" Matt asked.

"The Intergalactic Endeavour defectors request to live," Brigadier Tenn said, "the Protestors demand a meeting with us."

I looked to Matt, waiting for his decision. Then, he looked at me.

"What do you think?" he asked.

"What do you mean what do I think?" I scoffed, "you're Supreme Commander."

"And you're Supreme Commandress." He retorted.

I glanced at General Porter and Brigadier Tenn. The realization that I was actually in charge of the Intergalactic Endeavour had just fully hit me.

"Well... there's no harm in giving them that, right?" I said.

"Very well, we'll give them what they want," he said, "start making the arrangements... we'll see you tomorrow after we get some rest."

Matt grabbed my hand and turned sharply, pulling me out of the room behind him.

"Was that right?" I whispered.

"Why are you asking me?" he snorted, "you have just as much power as I do."

"Yeah, well," I sighed, "we're supposed to be working together."

"We are." He said.

He was acting odd, but there didn't seem to be a reason. I surmised that he must be tired from the journey. I was sure that he would be much better in the morning.

Though he was mostly back to normal the next day, I didn't have much time to enjoy it. I had never realized how much time and effort went into making peace until I had to do it. We had to have virtual meetings with Protestor leaders, during which we had to respond to all of their concerns about the Intergalactic Endeavour. The defectors had to be interrogated and then imprisoned in a secure prison off-planet. Then, we had to arrange the announcements and everything that went with it.

Five days after our return, everything seemed to be settled: the war had officially been won by the Intergalactic Endeavour and our official, public coronation ceremony was being planned for the first of Akua. The only thing that didn't seem to be settled was Matt. He was still incredibly reserved and distant, especially from me. It was absolutely infuriating, especially since I needed his support now more than ever.

"What's wrong?" I asked.

"What do you mean?" he frowned.

"You've been super weird lately." I said.

"I haven't." he argued.

"You have." I retorted.

He brushed me off and walked away.

"I had planned to kill you, you know." I snapped.

Matt turned around to face me, his brows furrowed. I hadn't really meant to blurt that out, especially not like that, but I desperately wanted his full attention again.

"What?" he asked.

"When I killed Diu," I told him, "The weapon I had... it was meant for you."

He looked absolutely crushed, which was exactly what I expected. My words were not necessarily meant to wound him, though I knew that my asperity would catch his attention. My foremost purpose now was to confess, to get the guilt off my chest, and to be completely transparent with him.

"I love you," I said, "I've loved you for a long time... maybe not as long as you've loved me, but it's not less strong."

"Why are you telling me this?" he scoffed, stepping closer.

He was getting angry and flustered, which was the perfect combination of emotions to get him to listen attentively.

"I don't love you more than God, or the purpose God gave me," I replied, "that's why I'm telling you this."

"And what is your purpose?" he snapped, coming even closer.

"I'm meant to rule the galaxy, to help it," I said, "I always have been... with or without you."

He turned around abruptly and took a deep breath. He was tense and his fists were clenched at his sides.

"Well, what would you rather do?" he inquired shakily.

"What do you mean by that?" I asked.

"Would you rather rule with me or without me?" he questioned.

He sounded as if he was clenching his teeth, but not in anger. I had hit a nerve – a vital nerve.

"I'd rather rule with you, of course." I breathed.

Matt turned around so quickly that it made me jump. He was holding back tears, that much was evident.

"Then why tell me all of this?" he asked.

"Because I want to be honest with you," I answered, "and I don't want to feel guilty anymore. And... and I don't want to feel distant from you anymore."

A deep chuckle emitted from him, and he looked up at the ceiling. I waited for his response, curiosity permeating my brain.

"That's the real reason then," he chuckled, "you think I'm distant and you're trying to get my attention."

I frowned at him, considering his playful expression. Perhaps that was one of the reasons, but certainly not the main one.

"Well, perhaps we need *real* distance," he smirked, "I'll see you at our coronation."

Matt walked out the door, leaving me alone in the penthouse. I had half a mind to go after him but decided against it. Maybe he was right, maybe we did need real, physical distance for a while. Perhaps we even needed permanent distance from each other.

On the morning of my coronation, which was to be televised galaxy wide, I was dressed in one of the most beautiful and regal gowns I had ever seen. The gown itself was the same shade of blue as the dress I had joined the Intergalactic Endeavour in. The sleeves flowed from the neckline, creating a sort of cape which flowed behind me. The dress was beautiful and intricate: I truly looked like the Supreme Commandress of the Intergalactic Endeavour.

Though I was nervous for the public coronation, I was more nervous to see Matt again. We had been apart for five days with absolutely no communication. In all honesty, I didn't know if he wanted to see me or if I wanted to see him. There was no way for me to know where our relationship was.

When I first saw him at the coronation, he was at the other end of the room, wearing a suit in a shade of grey which complemented my dress. He did not make eye contact with me, just looked straight ahead. It seemed that my hopes for a reconciliation had been completely and utterly dashed.

"Supreme Commander and Supreme Commandress," the preacher said, "please come forward."

Matt and I walked towards each other, still never making direct eye contact. We met in the middle aisle, then turned and walked towards the stage. The preacher reached out his hands, which each of us took as we ascended the stairs to the stage.

There was no official crowning, despite the ceremony's label as a coronation. Instead, the preacher, the chosen religious official of the organization, wrapped a silver belt around me, and a gold belt around him, our ranks embroidered into them, around our waists. The preacher then read out our full, official titles.

As soon as he was done reading our titles to the crowd, we turned to face them and waited for their applause to end. General Porter had, thankfully, drilled the entire process into my head, so I knew what happened next, despite not being able to practice with Matt. We would take each other's hands and walk together out of the room, right into a group of security guards who would escort us back to our penthouse.

The applause ended and I reached my hand out towards Matt. Propriety dictated that I did not look to him in this instance, but I was almost tempted to when I did not feel his hand take mine immediately. Once he did take my hand, I sighed in relief.

"Astraella." Matt said.

I looked over at him, thinking that I had done something wrong and embarrassed both of us. Instead of criticizing me, though, he knelt before me. I frowned as I looked down at him, wondering what he was doing in the midst of such an important ceremony.

"I started falling for you when you cared for me while I was sick," he said, "and I knew that I loved you the night we returned to base. I've wanted to ask you this since then, but I knew I should wait for the perfect moment."

I was starting to comprehend what he was leading up to, but I was still in a state of shock.

"Astraella Ne'ani Wander, Supreme Commandress of the Intergalactic Endeavour," he smiled, "will you marry me?"

The crowd erupted into applause as tears began to stream down my cheeks. I knew there was so much more to be done before we could settle down, but I knew that our amalgamation was inevitable. We were more than romantic partners now, we were colleagues, forever and ever. There was no other answer for me to give.

"Yes," I nodded, "I will marry you."

The crowd roared around us as Matt rose and wrapped his arms around me. As the crowd calmed, Matt took my hand and raised in triumphantly in the air. It was apparent to me now that this was not just an expression of our love, but also a show of power. I was proud of him; he was starting to think more and more like me every day. We were going to become a force to be reckoned with.

Chapter Eleven: The Force

"Do you understand now?" Matt asked as we entered the penthouse.

"Understand what?" I returned.

"Why I was so distant?" he chortled.

"Wait a minute." I frowned.

Suddenly, it all started to make sense: why he had taken so long after my hospital release to get me to Ai'Windel, why he'd been so upset when we were called back, why he had been so weird and distant when we'd returned.

"You... you were going to propose on Ai'Windel," I said, "weren't you?"

"You almost had to wait until our next trip there," he grinned, "but your parents urged me to propose at the coronation."

Emotions overtook me and I ran to Matt's arms, embracing him tightly. I was so excited to marry him, so happy my family approved of him, and so anxious to start officially ruling by his side as Supreme Commandress. If this all kept up, my life would be near-perfect.

The year following our coronation was a blur of meetings, law-writing, promotions, and treaties. We made much progress and succeeded in bringing practically universal peace under our rule, which we carried out under the watchful eye of God. With all of our responsibilities, we had no time to plan a wedding or any of the accompanying engagement obligations of a Supreme Commander and Supreme Commandress. In fact, it wasn't until our first annual address that I even really thought of our engagement.

"It has been one year since the engagement," one report called out to us, "is there any news on the upcoming engagement party? Or the wedding, for that matter?"

"We are still in the early planning stages." I smiled.

After that, no one really inquired about our relationship. We went back to our penthouse that night, both exhausted from the address and the ensuing interrogation.

"What do you think?" Matt asked.

"Of?" I sighed, my fatigue overtaking me.

"The question the red-haired reporter asked us." He replied.

"Which question?" I inquired.

"About the engagement and the wedding." He said.

"Oh, I didn't think much of it," I shrugged, "it's natural that they'd all be curious about it. It will be a big event when it happens."

"But... do you think we should get started on the planning?" he pressed.

I turned and regarded him carefully.

"We're not stable yet," I said, "we need to wait at least another year... to make sure all the progress we've made is secure."

"Are you going to keep pushing it off?" he demanded.

"What do you mean?" I frowned.

"Do you really want to marry me?" he asked.

"You know I do," I answered, "but what we're doing is important."

"They'll think we're divided," he said, "that we're weak. 'Every kingdom divided itself is brought to desolation, and every city or house divided against itself will not stand', remember?"

"I know." I sighed.

I bit my lip, searching for a solution.

"Here, this is what we'll do," I said, "we will begin planning the engagement party this year and celebrate it on Alze 10th of next year. That will keep them occupied until 5022, at the least."

"And what then?" he questioned.

"I expect we'll have the bridal gala and the groom's party the following year," I listed, "then we'll marry the next year. We'll be married in Alze 5024."

"You'll be 29 years," he said, "and I'll be nearly 45 years. Do we really want to wait that long?"

"I told you," I snapped, "we have more to do. We need more time before we settle down."

He stepped back, a pained look on his face. I realized immediately how he had taken what I had said.

"Listen, we've known each other... what?" I said, "a year and a half? That's it. Most people wouldn't have been engaged at this point anyways. We're ahead of the curve, so let's take our time."

He didn't say anything else to me, just stared at me for a moment and then left the room. I knew that what he thought I'd meant had hurt him, but I didn't have the energy to go after him. After all, we had much more to do the next day. I couldn't waste my sleeping hours on him, not right now.

I woke up early the next morning with an all too familiar nauseous feeling in my stomach. I ran to the bathroom just in time to regurgitate what little food I had eaten the previous day. I coughed and tried in vain to pull my hair back out of my face.

"Here." Matt whispered.

He gently pulled my hair back and held it there until I was somewhat back to normal.

"You okay?" he asked, his voice soft and scratchy from sleep.

"How did you hear me?" I returned.

He only shrugged.

"I'm sorry," I said, "I didn't mean to wake you."

"It's okay." He replied.

I took my hair from his hands and tied it back.

"Thanks." I said.

He nodded in acknowledgement.

"Are we... okay?" I asked.

"Aren't we always?" he chuckled.

I smiled in response, my stomach still feeling weak.

"I didn't want you to get sick over this," he said, "you know I hate when that happens."

"I'm sorry." I responded.

"It's not your fault," he sighed, "you know that. I just... feel bad."

"Don't." I shook my head.

His eyes crinkled at the corners as he pushed a stray piece of hair behind my ear. Once I felt well enough to stand, I reached my hands out for him. Following our usual routine, he helped me up and slowly walked me back to bed.

"We've got a lot to do," I noted, "should we try to get a couple more hours of sleep before we go?"

I reached my hand out towards him. Hesitantly, he climbed into bed next to me. We slept tumultuously for a short time, then arose for our full day of work. We soon returned to our normal days, which was only broken up by our engagement party announcement nine days later.

Matt and I did very little in the way of planning our engagement party. Other than the guest list and a few superficial details, we made very few decisions. I didn't mind, since I much preferred to focus on my work rather than on fickle things like parties, but it did seem to bother Matt a bit.

The only thing I cared about was that my family was coming to see me. We visited each other fairly often, but the visits were short because I was so busy all the time. With the engagement party, they had an excuse to come stay for an extended period of time and I had an excuse to get away from work.

The engagement party was bland, but it allowed me to focus on the guests, specifically my family. They rarely came to our base because it was so unsafe for them, so it was nice to have them with me instead of having to travel back to them. I did like going home to Ai'Windel, but every time I was there now, I was overwhelmed with the stress of what I was missing on base.

One year later, my family was back again for my bridal gala. I had more time to plan this party, and it was more personalized to me, which meant that I enjoyed it significantly more. Still, I kept my focus on my family. That was, I did, until a few unfamiliar guests crashed the party.

"Excuse me," an attendant approached them, "could I have your names please?"

"The Diu family." One of the guests answered.

Everyone had heard their response, and everyone turned their heads. The Diu family had been exiled after they had protested following Sara's death. I had told Matt to ignore them, that they could not possibly have any evidence, but he said that not doing something would give validation to their claims. I was too frightened of being found out to argue with him.

"The Diu family has been exiled to Olkana," I stood, "you are not welcome here."

"And yet, here we are." one of the women said.

"We are here to reveal the truth of Sara's death." Another man added.

My heart skipped a beat, my breath stopped, and I lost feeling in my limbs. I paused as a result of this, and I could tell that other people had noticed. Trying to regain my composure, I turned to the guards.

"Imprison them, and alert the Supreme Commander." I ordered.

The guards nodded and did as I had commanded. I stayed in my place, trying not to look too shaken.

"Don't mind them too much, Astra." Marsa patted my shoulder. "I can't believe there are still people out there attacking the Intergalactic Endeavour," Sofi added, "especially after all you and Matticas have done."

I nodded my head, unsure of what to say, and unsure of my ability to speak. Marsa and Sofi led me towards a couch and helped me sit down.

"The Supreme Commander will be here soon." A guard informed us.

I nodded once more.

"Don't stress yourself," my mother said, sitting next to me, "you'll make yourself ill."
"I know." I replied.

Matt walked in not long after the guard had announced his imminent arrival.

“What happened?” he asked, kneeling before me.

“Sara’s family,” I told him, “They got back... somehow.”

“That... how could that have happened?” he scoffed, “they’re supposed to be in a work camp on Olkana.”

“I know.” My voice cracked.

Matt took my hands in his and squeezed them tightly.

“We’ll keep them imprisoned here, where we can watch them,” he said, “we’ll put them in the highest security prison, we’ll have them under constant guard... and we’ll figure out how they got back.”

As tears welled in my eyes, I stood and ran towards the penthouse. I was ashamed and frightened, and I didn’t want my family or anyone else to see me like that.

"What's wrong?" Matt asked, entering the penthouse only moments after I had.

"If they're here, they've already reaped doubts in the minds of others," I trembled, "people are going to know... people are going to find out what I did."

"What we did." Matt corrected.

"I'm the one who killed her!" I shouted.

I realized afterwards that I should not have confessed my crimes so loudly. I collapsed into Matt's arms, shaking and sobbing.

"Hush, hush," Matt whispered, "it's okay."

"What will we do?" I asked.

"Aren't you the one who usually comes up with plans?" Matt chuckled.

"You're the one that's good at *these* plans." I replied.

He stroked my hair as a laugh rumbled through his chest.

"We'll imprison them, as I said," he declared, "give a speech condemning their actions, then see how it goes."

Though the party had been ruined, my family agreed to stay with me until things settled down. We implemented Matt's plan immediately and waited for the aftermath. The outcome of our actions was not as disastrous as it had been following Uxe's execution, but it still wasn't good.

Following his speech, conspiracy theories over how and why Sara Diu had died began to spread. These theories bred doubt, which turned to discontent, which turned to anger. Soon enough, there were riots throughout the galaxy. I had been foolish to expect eternal peace in our ephemeral galaxy, but I could not deny that I had hoped for it.

Matt suggested that we go into hiding and allow the riots the quell themselves. After seeing the violence of the riots, the other officers in the Intergalactic Endeavour officers agreed. My family and I would return to Ai'Windel to gather our belongings, then immediately return to Seva. As soon as we were back, all travel to and from Seva would be banned. We would be on full lockdown on the planet until everything was calm again.

The lockdown was a welcome change for me. Though I missed visiting Ai'Windel, I loved Seva, and I was happy to be there. I was even more happy to be locked in with Matt and my family. The riots were being controlled by the generals, brigadiers, and colonels, leaving Matt and I with an excess of free time.

However, the riots continued to grow. The riot leaders had died in skirmishes between our forces and theirs, bringing sympathy and support to their side. When Sara Diu's father killed himself in the prison on the anniversary of his daughter's death, it brought even more outrage. Some even believed that we had killed him.

Any and all media was shut down after Sara's father's death. This decision proved to be for the best when Sara's mother killed herself a few weeks later. Sara's siblings and cousins were placed on suicide watch, which also served the purpose of making sure they couldn't get messages out.

"We need to do something," General Porter said, "it's been a year, and it hasn't died down."

"We need a distraction." The newly appointed General Tenn agreed.

I looked at Matt, watching his expressions carefully as I spoke.

"Well, we had planned to marry this year," I said, "that's probably out of the question now, but we could announce a wedding date for next year."

"That could work," General Tenn replied, "everyone will be so excited about the wedding that they'll stop caring about the rioting."

"And it will be the first announcement from you two since Sugsa." General Porter nodded.

"So?" I asked Matt.

"Let's do it." He smiled.

On Alze 20, 5024, we took to the beautifully decorated Intergalactic Endeavour stage. Per Tenn and Porter's instructions, we had no audience, just a few cameras approved by the organization. Matt and I were to share the announcement equally, to display a unified and strong front.

"Good morning to the galaxy," Matt began, "we wish you peace in this tumultuous time."

"We come before you today," I continued, "to announce something we know you have all been waiting for."

General Tenn had pushed for excessive usage of the word "we", as she thought it would reinforce our unity.

"Supreme Commandress Astraella Ne'ani Wander," Matt said, "and I, Supreme Commander Matticas Daviad Damiran, have set the date for our wedding."

"We will wed on Alze 20, 5025," I announced, "on the Intergalactic Base in Seva."

"We continue to pray for peace and love," Matt added, "as we prepare for our wedding."

"Thank you." We finished in unison.

We walked off the stage, hand-in-hand and hoping the distraction would work. Not long after our announcement, we saw the result of our distraction. Many of the citizens had taken the bait and begun to theorize on the wedding and create memorabilia themed to our nuptials. Others, the more strong-willed ones, continued to push for rioting and resistance.

Soon enough, these cries for opposition were drowned out by chatter about our wedding. We released updates every so often, trying to keep the momentum going for as long as possible. With every piece of information released came a new wave of excitement from the people of the galaxy. We even allowed for travel to and from Seva to resume, to allow artisans and designers from all over the galaxy to help with the wedding planning.

The only downside to this was that our personal lives were highly publicized now. Our romance and our wedding entranced people, so we had to make the sacrifice. Still, we found time to be alone together.

"I want to design your wedding dress for you." Matt said one night.

"Why?" I chuckled nervously.

"I knew I loved you after the first ball we attended together," he told me, "You looked so beautiful in that dress and I knew as soon as I saw you that I wanted to marry you in a dress just like that."

"Alright, I'll give you a chance," I laughed, "but I just want you to know that I'm already having a wedding dress designed... so you'll probably have to settle for designing my reception dress."

"As long as I get to see you in a dress like that again." He kissed my forehead.

"What? You can't just wait until our honeymoon?" I giggled.

Chapter Twelve: The Amalgamation

Matt gave me the dress on his 45th birthday. The top portion of the dress was made of what seemed to be solid gold feathers. The bottom portion of the dress was also gold but was loose, unlike the feathered portion. A long, vertical piece in the bodice had been left open, presumably to display the skin underneath it. The dress met at the neck, giving the appearance of a necklace. It truly was a dress fit for a Supreme Commandress.

"What do you think?" he asked.

"I think you shouldn't be giving me presents for *your* birthday." I laughed.

"It's for me, too," he shrugged, "plus, your birthday is too close to our wedding."

I tried to think of a clever response but couldn't.

"You don't like it?" he asked sadly.

"I love it, Matt," I said, "I can't wait to wear it for the reception."

"Not the ceremony?" he inquired.

"I told you; I have another dress for the ceremony," I smiled, "the groom is not supposed to see the ceremony dress until the ceremony."

"Well, at least put it on for my birthday." He said.

"No, I'm gonna save it," I giggled, "but I do have something for you."

As soon as Matt had told me how much he'd liked the dress I'd worn to our first ball together, I'd put it away for an occasion like this.

"What do you think?" I asked, turning in front of him.

"It's even more beautiful now," he answered, "you fill it out better."

"Really?" I grinned.

He stood and crossed slowly over to me, his eyes roaming over me.

"You're gorgeous." He said.

"I'll be even more gorgeous at our wedding." I smiled.

"Oh?" he raised an eyebrow, "what does your dress look like?"

"Pretty." I smirked.

With that, I turned on my heel and made my way back to my bedroom.

"Come on," Matt pleaded, "just give me one detail!"

"We have four months left until the wedding," I replied, "wait."

"Please!" he whined.

I giggled and quickened my pace as I heard him running after me. He grabbed me, picking me up and spinning me around.

"I love you." He whispered.

"I love you too," I said, "happy birthday."

A little less than a month later, I turned 30. It felt very surreal for me to reach such a milestone in the middle of riots and wedding preparation. It felt even more surreal to be at the end of my third decade of life. However, I had no time to deal with the surrealness of it, because my wedding was 13 days later.

On Alze 20, 5025, the galaxy fell silent. I had been separated from Matt and the rest of the Intergalactic Endeavour for the past week, but I was acutely aware of the number of cameras and reporters surrounding the venue. I had been literally shaking since Alze 19, but I was trying to calm down so I wouldn't get sick on my wedding day.

Attendants assigned to me by Matt dressed me for the ceremony. My ceremony dress was white and heavy, weighed down by the myriads of precious stones and jewels which adorned it. The largest of the stones formed a collar which spanned from my neck to the bottom of my chest. The smaller ones were sewn throughout the dress, forming diagonal lines which met at my right hip. From the midsection of the dress flowed two panels, one on either side of my hips, which puffed out to the side and dragged on the floor behind me. Covering the entirety of the back half of the dress was a matching cape which was attached to the collar of the dress.

My hair had been left down, the blonde curls hitting just below my hips. On top of my head was placed a jeweled cap which matched my dress. Over this cap, I wore a silver tiara adorned with silver and diamond stars. At the end of my dressing, the attendants attached a circular piece which was adorned with matching stars to the upper back of my dress. It looked like a halo surrounding me.

"I look..." I said, considering myself in the mirror, "celestial.... ethereal."

“Is that good, Supreme Commandress?” an attendant asked.

“That’s exactly how a Supreme Commandress should look,” I smiled, “in my opinion, at least.”

“Shall we show your family in, then, Supreme Commandress?” the other inquired.

I nodded, still looking over myself in the mirror.

“You look beautiful.” Marsa said.

“I was thinking more along the lines of ‘otherworldly,’” I chuckled, “but thank you.”

The rest of my family shuffled in with their own compliments, then began the familial wedding preparations. Under my head cap, my mother pinned a veil which split down the middle in order to showcase the starred halo piece of my dress. The veil was even longer than my dress and made walking more difficult. Marsa and Sofi helped by each grabbing one side of the veil.

My father pinned a separate veil to the front of my hair so that it covered my face. Finally, my parents held out the box which contained my Wander family ring. I took it from the box and slid it onto my ring finger, noting the way it shined in the light. I rarely wore my family ring, so it was an unfamiliar sight and feel for me.

"Ready?" my mother asked, extending her hand.

I nodded, taking her hand in my right and my father's hand in my left. Sofi and Marsa followed, still holding my veil. Olver brought up the back, carrying the box that would hold my family ring once I was officially married.

My breath quickened as I began to think ahead to the ceremony and the following events. I was more nervous now than I had been the entire planning process, as I became more aware of what could go awry. Nearly everyone in the galaxy would be watching me, picking me apart and remembering every detail for news reports later in the day; how could I not be anxious?

"Breathe deeply." My mother reminded me as we began to walk towards the ceremony hall.

I took the deepest breath I could muster.

"Calm down." She added

I tried to follow her advice.

"Focus on Matticas," she continued, "focus on your love, not anything external."

"Is that what you did?" I asked, turning towards her.

She nodded and smiled.

"You can't possibly trip," Sofi chimed in, "you've got four people keeping you up."

"And if you do trip," Olver said, "I will distract them with my beautiful hair."

A chuckle emitted from everyone in the party. As we neared the ceremony hall, we fell silent. Two guards stood on either side of the double doors, prepared to escort us inside.

"Are you ready, Supreme Commandress?" one of them asked.

I nodded, and the guard pressed a button by the door. I could see the lights inside the hall dimming and music began to play. A few moments later, the guards opened the door and began walking down the aisle.

"Deep breath." My mother said.

I obeyed her and took one more deep breath before we stepped inside the hall. It took everything in me not to gasp as we stepped inside. Projected on the vaulted ceiling and paned walls was our beautiful, blueish galaxy. The silvery white stars and diverse planets dotted the blue, and supernovas accentuated the scene.

My mother squeezed my hand rebukingly, pulling me back into the present. I tilted my chin down, bringing my eyes from the ceiling to the aisle before me. Hundreds of people sat in the pews surrounding the aisle, watching me diligently. At the end of the aisle was Matt, dressed in gold and black. His brown eyes sparkled with happy tears and the sight extracted the same kind of tears from my own eyes. We chuckled at ourselves, so overwhelmed with emotion that tears streamed down our cheeks.

The walk down the aisle seemed to take forever. Had my parents not been holding me in place, I would have run towards him. I no longer wanted all this publicity, all this pomp and circumstance. All I wanted was to share this day with him, to celebrate our love.

Finally, we got to the end of the aisle, illuminated in the twinkling blue light of the planet lights above us. In perfect unison, my parents lifted my hands and pressed a kiss to my knuckles. My mother gave my hand to Matt first, then joined my father at my left. Together, they removed my family ring from my ring finger. Olver scurried to their side and shakily held out the box, which they placed the ring in.

Tearfully, my parents placed my left hand into Matt's, signifying my leaving their family and beginning my own. My sisters fixed my veil and gown into position, then left with the rest of my family. They sat down in the front pew on my right, sniffling at regular intervals.

"Welcome to all gathered here," the preacher's voice echoed, "we gather to witness and celebrate the union of Supreme Commander Matticas Daviad Damiran and Supreme Commandress Astraella Ne'ani Wander."

Light applause emitted from those surrounding us.

"Astraella Wander, do you commit yourself to Matticas Damiran from now until your death?" the preacher asked.

"I do." I responded.

"Matticas Damiran, do you commit yourself to Astraella Wander from now until your death?" the preacher repeated.

"I do." Matt smiled.

I smiled and giggled softly in an attempt to suppress my gleeful tears.

"Astraella Wander, do you promise to love Matticas Damiran," the preacher continued, "to stay by his side regardless of the circumstances, to support him come what may, and be bound to him under the law of God?"

"I do." I nodded.

"Matticas Damiran, do you promise to love Astraella Wander," the preacher repeated, "to stay by her side regardless of the circumstances, to support her come what may, and be bound to her under the law of God?"

"I do." He said.

"Matticas Daviad Damiran and Astraella Ne'ani Wander have made the solemn vows," the preacher announced, "and may now place upon each other their new family rings."

The preacher turned, retrieved our family rings from a box, then handed them to us. Matt shakily slipped my ring onto my ring finger, and I did the same for him.

"This man and this woman are now joined as a married couple," the preacher continued, "according to the power vested in me by God and the Intergalactic Endeavour."

He took our left hands, now adorned with our family rings, in his.

"Matticas, Astraella, bear witness to the love of God in this galaxy," he said, "I now pronounce you husband and wife. You may now seal your marriage with a kiss."

That was it; we were now officially married under Divine Law and Intergalactic Law. We kissed, sealing our marriage, as the crowd erupted into applause. We broke our kiss after what seemed like forever, both smiling and crying with delight.

"Do you two wish to announce your new family name at this time?" the preacher asked once the crowd had settled.

"Yes." We responded in unison.

The preacher nodded and motioned for us to step forward and make the announcement. Matt took my left hand in his and we stepped forward to the edge of the stage. We looked at each other, nodded, then turned back to the audience.

"Our new family name," we said together, "is Wandamiran."

There were four choices given to couples who were to be married in terms of family names. They could take the first partner's name or the second partner's name, not change their family names at all, or create a new one, either combining their existing family names or inventing a completely different one. We had chosen to go with the fourth choice, combining our family names to create the most concordant new family name.

We must have done a good job choosing our new family name, because everyone applauded once again. They stood as we walked out, still applauding enthusiastically. My parents followed us out with General Porter and Tenn, who were taking the place of Matt's late parents. Once we were outside the ceremonial hall and the doors were closed, we turned to each other.

"We're married!" I exclaimed, hopping happily.

"We're married." he echoed, grinning.

"And now it's time to get ready for the reception." My mother interjected.

"Yes, of course," I responded, "I'll see you later, my dearest husband."

I giggled and kissed him quickly, then left with my family. They all chatted happily, their excitement surrounding the reception fogging their emotions over the ceremony. We gathered in the same room we had been in before the ceremony, but it seemed more open and inviting.

While my family chatted, I went back to change into the golden dress that Matt had gotten made for me. I put on a golden star crown to elevate my ensemble, then rejoined my family. They all turned to look at me when I entered, their chattering stopping for a moment.

"You look beautiful." Marsa smiled.

"Thank you." I replied.

After showering me with compliments, my family changed into their own outfits for the reception. There was a decent span of time between the ceremony and the reception, so we all had time to relax after changing. This served me well, since I especially needed time to relax today. I was so stressed about doing everything right, and everything seemed to be going so quickly that I couldn't even comprehend it.

"I can't believe you're married." Sofi mused.

"I know." I replied, holding my left hand up in front of me.

"Wandamiran, huh?" Olver said, "I like Wander myself."

"We wanted to each share the family name equally." I shrugged.

"Shall we get going?" my mother interrupted.

I felt overdressed as we walked towards the ballroom for the reception. Matt and I'd had the most say in the planning of the reception, since there were no traditions dictating it.

"So, what do you have in store for us at the reception?" my mother inquired.

"Just wait until you see it," I grinned, "it will be like dancing in the sky."

Though I was confident in our planning skills, I could never have envisioned what waited for me at the reception. The attendants had done a better job than I could have hoped. The floor glowed blue, with white stars adorning it. Surrounding the walkways and the dancefloor were fluffy white tufts of fabric which looked like clouds. From the ceiling hung glowing, golden and crystal bulbs which bathed the room in soft light.

There were tables and tables of food, most of which was gold. In between each section of food were roses, painted the same shade of gold. Our wedding cake was three-tiered, with the bottom and top layers colored white and gold. The middle layer matched the plate underneath; navy blue with golden constellations.

"Shall we?" Matt's voice boomed above me.

I blinked, snapping out of my beauty-induced trance. My family had shifted towards their table and everyone's eyes were on us, the newlyweds. I took his hand and allowed him to pull me to the cloud-covered dance floor. We swayed and spun to the music, our eyes twinkling with the lights. Matt wore a silver suit to contrast my gold dress, continuing our silver and gold theme.

"You look gorgeous." Matt complimented me.

"And you look handsome." I returned.

"Are you hungry?" he whispered, chuckling.

"Yes," I sighed, "when does this song end?"

He laughed and continued leading me through the dance. After what seemed like forever, the song ended, and other couples began to fill the dance floor. Matt and I danced for a while longer, then snuck off towards the nearest food table. There were gold macarons, champagne gel cubes, gold and white chocolate strawberries, gold strawberries, gold apples, gold cupcakes, gold gel stars, clear golden pie, golden spun sugar, and golden iced cream. I tried everything, curious to see how my ideas actually tasted.

"Everything is so beautiful." I noted.

"You planned it well." Matt said.

"You helped me well." I nudged him.

We made our way to the head table, where our throne-like chairs sat. We lounged back into our chairs, eating our food as we watched our guests celebrating our marriage. The food was delicious, the scenery was celestial, and everything seemed to be perfect. The only issue I encountered as I relaxed was my anxiety for later in the night.

The reception did not end until early the next morning. Matt and I spent the evening eating, dancing, relaxing, and socializing with our guests. In reality, it felt more like a business function than a romantic wedding. It was not until we absconded to one of the small, hilly islands in the middle of the water which surrounded the base that we got to truly comprehend our wedding.

"Are you tired?" Matt asked as he helped me out of my reception dress.

"Not too tired." I shrugged.

"We don't have to." He said.

"I know," I replied, "but we should."

"Why?" he snorted.

"Because you want to," I said, "and you deserve it."

"It's not about deserving," he chortled, "it's about what we *both* want."

I'd known Matt for more than five years now, but he still managed to surprise me with his kindness and consideration. Of course, he was a bit oblivious when it came to the masses and government, but when he dealt with people directly, he was truly the kindest man I had ever met.

"I wouldn't have married you if I didn't want you." I chuckled.

I kissed him.

Epilogue

Since our wedding, we had tried many times to have children. After a couple of years, we went to a doctor for advice, only to be told that I was unable to have children. This made the future of the Intergalactic Endeavour uncertain, since under usual circumstances we would train up our children in the Intergalactic Endeavour and leave the highest ranking one in charge once we were ready to retire. Other than that, it didn't really affect us. Neither of us had really wanted children, instead choosing to focus on faith, work, and each other.

The future rulers would instead essentially be determined by God. Preference would, of course, be given to the potential future children of General Porter, General Tenn, and my younger siblings. Still, everyone in the future had a relatively equal chance of becoming the next leaders of the Intergalactic Endeavour. I only prayed that the future leaders would do well in upholding and improving the organization we had built.

Marsa had met a man named Kristof, the son of Intergalactic Endeavour employees from Manno, at our wedding. They had kept in touch for a couple of years before Marsa went to live on Manno with him. They stayed there for a year before Kristof's parents convinced him to take a job with the Intergalactic Endeavour and move to Seva. He and Marsa relocated to the base on Seva, so I was able to see them more often.

With two daughters permanently residing in Seva, my parents and youngest two siblings began to spend more time on base. They still kept our family home in Ai'Windel, but they also took up a semi-permanent residence on base. This allowed them to be in attendance for the wedding of Kristof and Marsa, which occurred four years after their meeting.

Olver met his love in Seva as well, falling for the daughter of one of the lower-ranking individuals in the Intergalactic Endeavour. Her name was Fawxi, and she was very pretty and classy, with beautiful, wavy, strawberry blonde hair. She was certainly one of the prettiest young women on base and had been courted by several others before Olver. Yet, no one seemed to catch her attention like Olver had.

It was possible that Olver and Fawxi had the most endearing love story. They had met a few days after Fawxi's family moved onto the base, and it was clear from their first meeting that they were meant to be. Their eyes had locked, and they had both blushed, leaning ever so subtly towards each other the entire time.

Olver proposed to Fawxi a little over two years after their first meeting, which surprised absolutely no one. They had the most marvelous connection, and it was inevitable that they'd marry. Their wedding was simple, but the most romantic thing I'd ever seen.

Sofi remained unmarried well after Olver's wedding. In fact, she remained completely unattached to any one person well after Marsa and Olver had their first children. She remained unmarried even after my parents adopted their fifth child, a little girl named Daphtha. Sofi had several prospects, but she never wanted to commit herself to any of them. Instead, she enjoyed stringing them along and receiving their affections. It was comical to those of us on the outside, but I was sure it was miserable for her suitors.

"Will she every marry?" Marsa remarked one cool summer evening.

The rest of us chuckled as we watched Sofi show off to her 2nd favorite boyfriend.

"I think she'll fall in love, truly, one day." Kristof mused.

"I doubt it," Olver snorted, "I think she's meant to be polyamorous."

"I don't know," Fawxi argued, "maybe one day."

"I hope she will," I sighed, "I'd like to better our chances of having someone from the Wander line rule the Intergalactic Endeavour."

"I think it's good she's having fun." My mother said.

I looked back out towards my youngest sibling, hugging her boyfriend.

"It would seem that she's happy." Matt agreed.

We all considered Sofi once more. She twirled around, holding her boyfriend's hand loosely. He watched her in wonderment, as all her admirers did.

"I guess, apart from the really important stuff," I said, "that's all that matters... that we're all happy."

As the years continued on, we continued to be happy. All of us had found different sources of happiness, but it was happiness, nonetheless. The only prayer we all had now was that our happiness and the galaxy's peace would continue on for many, many years.

www.ingramcontent.com/pod-product-compliance
Lightning Source LLC
LaVergne TN
LVHW100521110826
845146LV00002B/724

* 9 7 9 8 9 8 5 5 1 9 5 5 6 *